P9-CQL-098

Coronado

ALSO BY DENNIS LEHANE

A Drink Before the War

Darkness, Take My Hand

Sacred

Gone, Baby, Gone

Prayers for Rain

Mystic River

Shutter Island

Coronado

STORIES

DENNIS LEHANE

wm

WILLIAM MORROW
An Imprint of HarperCollins*Publishers*

AR **CASS COUNTY PUBLIC LIBRARY**
400 E. MECHANIC
HARRISONVILLE, MO 64701

0 0022 0485028 9

"ICU" originally appeared in the *Beloit Fiction Journal,* Spring 2004, vol. 17. "Gone Down to Corpus" originally appeared in *The Mighty Johns,* edited by Otto Penzler, published by New Millennium Press (July 2002). "Running Out of Dog" originally appeared in *Murder and Obsession,* 1999. "Until Gwen" appeared in *The Atlantic,* June 2004, and was adapted for the stage as *Coronado* in November 2005.

This book is a work of fiction. The characters, incidents, and dialogue are drawn from the author's imagination and are not to be construed as real. Any resemblance to actual events or persons, living or dead, is entirely coincidental.

CORONADO. Copyright © 2006 by Dennis Lehane. All rights reserved. Printed in the United States of America. No part of this book may be used or reproduced in any manner whatsoever without written permission except in the case of brief quotations embodied in critical articles and reviews. For information address HarperCollins Publishers, 10 East 53rd Street, New York, NY 10022.

HarperCollins books may be purchased for educational, business, or sales promotional use. For information please write: Special Markets Department, HarperCollins Publishers, 10 East 53rd Street, New York, NY 10022.

FIRST EDITION

Designed by Laura Kaeppel

Library of Congress Cataloging-in-Publication Data

Lehane, Dennis.
    Coronado : stories / Dennis Lehane.—1st ed.
      p. cm.
    ISBN-13: 978-0-06-113967-3
    ISBN-10: 0-06-113967-X
    I. Title.

PS3562.E426C67 2006
813'.54—dc22   2006044968

06 07 08 09 10 WBC/RRD 10 9 8 7 6 5 4 3 2 1

For Ann Rittenberg and Claire Wachtel

Contents

RUNNING OUT OF DOG

THIS THING WITH Blue and the dogs and Elgin Bern happened a while back, a few years after some of our boys—like
Elgin Bern and Cal Sears—came back from Vietnam, and a lot
of others—like Eddie Vorey and Carl Joe Carol, the Stewart
cousins—didn't. We don't know how it worked in other towns,
but that war put something secret in our boys who returned.
Something quiet and untouchable. You sensed they knew
things they'd never say, did things on the sly you'd never dis-
cover. Great cardplayers, those boys, able to bluff with the
best, let no joy show in their face no matter what they were
holding.

A small town is a hard place to keep a secret, and a small
southern town with all that heat and all those open windows is
an even harder place than most. But those boys who came back
from overseas, they seemed to have mastered the trick of privacy.
And the way it's always been in this town, you get a sizeable

crop of young, hard men coming up at the same time, they sort of set the tone.

So, not long after the war, we were a quieter town, a less trusting one (or so some seemed to think), and that's right when tobacco money and textile money reached a sort of critical mass and created construction money and pretty soon there was talk that our small town should maybe get a little bigger, maybe build something that would bring in more tourist dollars than we'd been getting from fireworks and pecans.

That's when some folks came up with this Eden Falls idea—a big carnival-type park with roller coasters and water slides and such. Why should all those Yankees spend all their money in Florida? South Carolina had sun too. Had golf courses and grapefruit and no end of KOA campgrounds.

So now a little town called Eden was going to have Eden Falls. We were going to be on the map, people said. We were going to be in all the brochures. We were small now, people said, but just you wait. Just you wait.

And that's how things stood back then, the year Perkin and Jewel Lut's marriage hit a few bumps and Elgin Bern took up with Shelley Briggs and no one seemed able to hold onto their dogs.

THE PROBLEM WITH dogs in Eden, South Carolina, was that the owners who bred them bred a lot of them. Or they allowed them to run free where they met up with other dogs of opposite gender and achieved the same result. This wouldn't have been so bad if Eden weren't so close to I-95, and if the dogs weren't in the habit of bolting into traffic and fucking up the bumpers of potential tourists.

The mayor, Big Bobby Vargas, went to a mayoral conference up in Beaufort, where the governor made a surprise appearance to tell everyone how pissed off he was about this dog thing. Lot of money being poured into Eden these days, the governor said, lot of steps being taken to change her image, and he for one would be goddamned if a bunch of misbehaving canines was going to mess all that up.

"Boys," he'd said, looking Big Bobby Vargas dead in the eye, "they're starting to call this state the Devil's Kennel 'cause of them pooch corpses along the interstate. And I don't know about you-all, but I don't think that's a real pretty name."

Big Bobby told Elgin and Blue he'd never heard anyone call it the Devil's Kennel in his life. Heard a lot worse, sure, but never that. Big Bobby said the governor was full of shit. But, being the governor and all, he was sort of entitled.

The dogs in Eden had been a problem going back to the twenties and a part-time breeder named J. Mallon Ellenburg who, if his arms weren't up to their elbows in the guts of the tractors and combines he repaired for a living, was usually lashing out at something—his family when they weren't quick enough, his dogs when the family was. J. Mallon Ellenburg's dogs were mixed breeds and mongrels and they ran in packs, as did their offspring, and several generations later, those packs still moved through the Eden night like wolves, their bodies stripped to muscle and gristle, tense and angry, growling in the dark at J. Mallon Ellenburg's ghost.

Big Bobby went to the trouble of measuring exactly how much of 95 crossed through Eden, and he came up with 2.8 miles. Not much really, but still an average of .74 dog a day or 4.9 dogs a week. Big Bobby wanted the rest of the state funds the governor was going to be doling out at year's end, and if that meant getting rid of five dogs a week, give or take, then that's what was going to get done.

"On the QT," he said to Elgin and Blue, "on the QT, what we going to do, boys, is set up in some trees and shoot every canine who gets within barking distance of that interstate."

Elgin didn't much like this "we" stuff. First place, Big Bobby'd said "we" that time in Double O's four years ago. This was before he'd become mayor, when he was nothing more than a county tax assessor who shot pool at Double O's every other night, same as Elgin and Blue. But one night, after Harlan and Chub Uke had roughed him up over a matter of some pocket change, and knowing that neither Elgin nor Blue was too fond of the Uke family either, Big Bobby'd said, "We going to settle those boys' asses tonight," and started running his mouth the minute the brothers entered the bar.

Time the smoke cleared, Blue had a broken hand, Harlan and Chub were curled up on the floor, and Elgin's lip was busted. Big Bobby, meanwhile, was hiding under the pool table, and Cal Sears was asking who was going to pay for the pool stick Elgin had snapped across the back of Chub's head.

So Elgin heard Mayor Big Bobby saying "we" and remembered the ten dollars it had cost him for that pool stick, and he said, "No, sir, you can count me out this particular enterprise."

Big Bobby looked disappointed. Elgin was a veteran of a foreign war, former Marine, a marksman. "Shit," Big Bobby said, "what good are you, you don't use the skills Uncle Sam spent good money teaching you?"

Elgin shrugged. "Damn, Bobby. I guess not much."

But Blue kept his hand in, as both Big Bobby and Elgin knew he would. All the job required was a guy didn't mind sitting in a tree who liked to shoot things. Hell, Blue was home.

ELGIN DIDN'T HAVE the time to be sitting up in a tree anyway. The past few months, he'd been working like crazy after they'd broke ground at Eden Falls—mixing cement, digging postholes, draining swamp water to shore up the foundation—with the real work still to come. There'd be several more months of drilling and bilging, spreading cement like cake icing, and erecting scaffolding to erect walls to erect facades. There'd be the hump-and-grind of rolling along in the dump trucks and drill trucks, the forklifts and cranes and industrial diggers, until the constant heave and jerk of them drove up his spine or into his kidneys like a corkscrew.

Time to sit up in a tree shooting dogs? Shit. Elgin didn't have time to take a piss some days.

And then on top of all the work, he'd been seeing Drew Briggs's ex-wife, Shelley, lately. Shelley was the receptionist at Perkin Lut's Auto Emporium, and one day Elgin had brought his Impala in for a tire rotation and they'd got to talking. She'd been divorced from Drew over a year, and they waited a couple of months to show respect, but after a while they began showing up at Double O's and down at the IHOP together.

Once they drove clear to Myrtle Beach together for the weekend. People asked them what it was like, and they said, "Just like the postcards." Since the postcards never mentioned the price of a room at the Hilton, Elgin and Shelley didn't mention that all they'd done was drive up and down the beach twice before settling in a motel a bit west in Conway. Nice, though; had a color TV and one of those switches turned the bathroom into a sauna if you let the shower run. They'd started making love in the sauna, finished up on the bed with steam coiling out from the bathroom and brushing their heels. Afterward, he pushed her hair back off her forehead and looked in her eyes and told her he could get used to this.

She said, "But wouldn't it cost a lot to install a sauna in your trailer?" then waited a full thirty seconds before she smiled.

Elgin liked that about her, the way she let him know he was still just a man after all, always would take himself too seriously, part of his nature. Letting him know she might be around to keep him apprised of that fact every time he did. Keep him from pushing a bullet into the breech of a thirty-aught-six, slamming the bolt home, firing into the flank of some wild dog.

Sometimes, when they'd shut down the site early for the day—if it had rained real heavy and the soil loosened near a foundation, or if supplies were running late—he'd drop by Lut's to see her. She'd smile as if he'd brought her flowers, say, "Caught boozing on the job again?" or some other smart-ass thing, but it made him feel good, as if something in his chest suddenly realized it was free to breathe.

Before Shelley, Elgin had spent a long time without a woman he could publicly acknowledge as his. He'd gone with Mae Shiller from fifteen to nineteen, but she'd gotten lonely while he was overseas, and he'd returned to find her gone from Eden, married to a boy up in South of the Border, the two of them working a corn-dog concession stand, making a tidy profit, folks said. Elgin dated some, but it took him a while to get over Mae, to get over the loss of something he'd always expected to have, the sound of her laugh and an image of her stepping naked from Cooper's Lake, her pale flesh beaded with water, having been the things that got Elgin through the jungle, through the heat, through the ticking of his own death he'd heard in his ears every night he'd been over there.

About a year after he'd come home, Jewel Lut had come to visit her mother, who still lived in the trailer park where Jewel had grown up with Elgin and Blue, where Elgin still lived. On her way out, she'd dropped by Elgin's and they'd sat out front of his trailer in some folding chairs, had a few drinks, talked about old times. He told her a bit about Vietnam, and she told him a bit about marriage. How it wasn't what you expected, how Perkin Lut might know a lot of things but he didn't know a damn sight about having fun.

There was something about Jewel Lut that sank into men's flesh the way heat did. It wasn't just that she was pretty, had a beautiful body, moved in a loose, languid way that made you picture her naked no matter what she was wearing. No, there was more to it. Jewel, never the brightest girl in town and not even the most charming, had something in her eyes that none of the women Elgin ever met had; it was a capacity for living, for taking moments—no matter how small or inconsequential—and squeezing every last thing you could out of them. Jewel gobbled up life, dove into it like it was a cool pond cut in the shade of a mountain on the hottest day of the year.

That look in her eyes—the one that never left—said, Let's have fun, goddammit. Let's eat. Now.

She and Elgin hadn't been stupid enough to do anything that night, not even after Elgin caught that look in her eyes, saw it was directed at him, saw she wanted to eat.

Elgin knew how small Eden was, how people loved to insinuate and pry and talk. So he and Jewel worked it out, a once-a-week thing mostly that happened down in Carlyle, at a small cabin had been in Elgin's family since before the War Between the States. There, Elgin and Jewel were free to partake of each other, squeeze and bite and swallow and inhale each other, to make love in the lake, on the porch, in the tiny kitchen.

They hardly ever talked, and when they did, it was about nothing at all, really—the decline in the quality of the meat at Billy's Butcher Shop, rumors that parking meters were going to be installed in front of the courthouse, if McGarrett and the rest of Five-O would ever put the cuffs on Wo Fat.

There was an unspoken understanding that he was free to date any woman he chose and that she'd never leave Perkin Lut. And that was just fine. This wasn't about love; it was about appetite.

Sometimes, Elgin would see her in town or hear Blue speak about her in that puppy-dog-love way he'd been speaking about her since high school, and he'd find himself surprised by the realization that he slept with this woman. That no one knew. That it could go on forever, if both of them remained careful, vigilant against the wrong look, the wrong tone in their voices when they spoke in public.

He couldn't entirely put his finger on what need she satisfied, only that he needed her in that lakefront cabin once a week, that it had something to do with walking out of the jungle alive, with the ticking of his own death he'd heard for a full year. Jewel was somehow reward for that, a fringe benefit. To be naked and spent with her atop him and seeing that look in her eyes that said she was ready to go again, ready to gobble him up like oxygen. He'd earned that by shooting at shapes in the night, pressed against those damp foxhole walls that never stayed shored up for long, only to come home to a woman who couldn't wait, who'd discarded him as easily as she would a once-favored doll she'd grown beyond, looked back upon with a wistful mix of nostalgia and disdain.

He'd always told himself that when he found the right woman, his passion for Jewel, his need for those nights at the lake, would disappear. And, truth was, since he'd been with Shelley Briggs, he and Jewel had cooled it. Shelley wasn't Perkin, he told Jewel; she'd figure it out soon enough if he left town once a week, came back with bite marks on his abdomen.

Jewel said, "Fine. We'll get back to it whenever you're ready."

Knowing there'd be a next time, even if Elgin wouldn't admit it to himself.

So Elgin, who'd been so lonely in the year after his discharge, now had two women. Sometimes, he didn't know what to think of that. When you were alone, the happiness of others boiled your insides. Beauty seemed ugly. Laughter seemed evil. The casual grazing of one lover's hand into another was enough to make you want to cut them off at the wrist. *I will never be loved,* you said. *I will never know joy.*

He wondered sometimes how Blue made it through. Blue,

who'd never had a girlfriend he hadn't rented by the half hour.
Who was too ugly and small and just plain weird to evoke anything
in women but fear or pity. Blue, who'd been carrying a torch for
Jewel Lut since long before she married Perkin and kept carrying it
with a quiet fever Elgin could only occasionally identify with. Blue,
he knew, saw Jewel Lut as a queen, as the only woman who existed
for him in Eden, South Carolina. All because she'd been nice to
him, pals with him and Elgin, back about a thousand years ago, before sex, before breasts, before Elgin or Blue had even the smallest
clue what that thing between their legs was for, before Perkin Lut
had come along with his daddy's money and his nice smile and his
bullshit stories about how many men he'd have killed in the war if
only the draft board had seen fit to let him go.

Blue figured if he was nice enough, kind enough, waited long
enough—then one day Jewel would see his decency, need to cling
to it.

Elgin never bothered telling Blue that some women didn't want
decency. Some women didn't want a nice guy. Some women, and
some men too, wanted to get into a bed, turn out the lights, and
feast on each other like animals until it hurt to move.

Blue would never guess that Jewel was that kind of woman, because she was always so sweet to him, treated him like a child really,
and with every friendly hello she gave him, every pat on the shoulder, every "What you been up to, old bud?" Blue pushed her further and further up the pedestal he'd built in his mind.

"I seen him at the Emporium one time," Shelley told Elgin. "He
just come in for no reason anyone understood and sat reading magazines until Jewel came in to see Perkin about something. And

Blue, he just stared at her. Just stared at her talking to Perkin in the showroom. When she finally looked back, he stood up and left."

Elgin hated hearing about, talking about, or thinking about Jewel when he was with Shelley. It made him feel unclean.

"Crazy love," he said to end the subject.

"Crazy something, babe."

Nights sometimes, Elgin would sit with Shelley in front of his trailer, listen to the cicadas hum through the scrawny pine, smell the night and the rock salt mixed with gravel; the piña colada shampoo Shelley used made him think of Hawaii, though he'd never been, and he'd think how their love wasn't crazy love, wasn't burning so fast and furious it'd burn itself out they weren't careful. And that was fine with him. If he could just get his head around this Jewel thing, stop seeing her naked and waiting and looking back over her shoulder at him in the cabin, then he could make something with Shelley. She was worth it. She might not be able to fuck like Jewel, and, truth be told, he didn't laugh as much with her, but Shelley was what you aspired to. A good woman, who'd be a good mother, who'd stick by you when times got tough. Sometimes he'd take her hand in his and hold it for no other reason but the doing of it. She caught him one night, some look in his eyes, maybe the way he tilted his head to look at her small white hand in his big brown one.

She said, "Damn, Elgin, if you ain't simple sometimes." Then she came out of her chair in a rush and straddled him, kissed him as if she were trying to take a piece of him back with her. She said, "Baby, we ain't getting any younger. You know?"

And he knew, somehow, at that moment why some men build

families and others shoot dogs. He just wasn't sure where he fit in the equation.

He said, "We ain't, are we?"

BLUE HAD BEEN Elgin's best buddy since either of them could remember, but Elgin had been wondering about it lately. Blue'd always been a little different, something Elgin liked, sure, but there was more to it now. Blue was the kind of guy you never knew if he was quiet because he didn't have anything to say or, because what he had to say was so horrible, he knew enough not to send it out into the atmosphere.

When they'd been kids, growing up in the trailer park, Blue used to be out at all hours because his mother was either entertaining a man or had gone out and forgotten to leave him the key. Back then, Blue had this thing for cockroaches. He'd collect them in a jar, then drop bricks on them to test their resiliency. He told Elgin once, "That's what they are—resilient. Every generation, we have to come up with new ways to kill 'em because they get immune to the poisons we had before." After a while, Blue took to dousing them in gasoline, lighting them up, seeing how resilient they were then.

Elgin's folks told him to stay away from the strange, dirty kid with the white-trash mother, but Elgin felt sorry for Blue. He was half Elgin's size even though they were the same age; you could place your thumb and forefinger around Blue's biceps and meet them on the other side. Elgin hated how Blue seemed to have only two pairs of clothes, both usually dirty, and how sometimes they'd pass his trailer together and hear the animal sounds coming from inside, the grunts and moans, the slapping of flesh. Half the time you couldn't tell if Blue's old lady was in there fucking or fighting. And always the sound of country music mingled in with all that animal noise, Blue's mother and her man of the moment listening to it on the transistor radio she'd given Blue one Christmas.

"On *my* fucking radio," Blue said once and shook his small head, the only time Elgin ever saw him react to what went on in that trailer.

Blue was a reader—knew more about science and ecology, about anatomy and blue whales and conversion tables than anyone Elgin knew. Most everyone figured the kid for a mute—hell, he'd been held back twice in fourth grade—but with Elgin he'd sometimes chat up a storm while they puffed smokes together down at the drainage ditch behind the park. He'd talk about whales, how they bore only one child, who they were fiercely protective of, but how if another child was orphaned, a mother whale would take it as her own, protect it as fiercely as she did the one she gave birth to. He told Elgin that sharks never slept, how electrical currents worked, what a depth charge was. Elgin, never much of a talker, just sat and listened, ate it up and waited for more.

The older they got, the more Elgin became Blue's protector, till finally, the year Blue's face exploded with acne, Elgin got in about two fights a day until there was no one left to fight. Everyone knew—they were brothers. And if Elgin didn't get you from the front, Blue was sure to take care of you from behind, like that time a can of acid fell on Roy Hubrist's arm in shop, or the time someone hit Carnell Lewis from behind with a brick, then cut his

Achilles tendon with a razor while he lay out cold. Everyone knew it was Blue, even if no one actually saw him do it.

Elgin figured with Roy and Carnell, they'd had it coming. No great loss. It was since Elgin'd come back from Vietnam, though, that he'd noticed some things and kept them to himself, wondered what he was going to do the day he'd know he had to do something.

There was the owl someone had set afire and hung upside down from a telephone wire, the cats who turned up missing in the blocks that surrounded Blue's shack off Route 11. There were the small pink panties Elgin had seen sticking out from under Blue's bed one morning when he'd come to get him for some cleanup work at a site. He'd checked the missing-persons reports for days, but it hadn't come to anything, so he'd just decided Blue had picked them up himself, fed a fantasy or two. He didn't forget, though, couldn't shake the way those panties had curled upward out of the brown dust under Blue's bed, seemed to be pleading for something.

He'd never bothered asking Blue about any of this. That never worked. Blue just shut down at times like that, stared off somewhere, as if something you couldn't hear was drowning out your words, something you couldn't see was taking up his line of vision. Blue, floating away on you, until you stopped cluttering up his mind with useless talk.

ELGIN WENT INTO town with Shelley so she could get her hair done at Martha's Unisex on Main. In Martha's, as Dottie Leeds gave Shelley a shampoo and rinse, Elgin felt like he'd stumbled into a chapel of womanhood. There was Jim Hayder's teenage daughter Sonny, getting one of those feathered cuts was growing popular these days, and several older women who still wore beehives, getting them reset or plastered or whatever they did to keep them up like that. There was Joylene Covens and Lila Sims having their nails done while their husbands golfed and the black maids watched their kids, and Martha and Dottie and Esther and Gertrude and Hayley dancing and flitting, laughing and chattering among the chairs, calling everyone "honey," and all of them—the young, the old, the rich, and Shelley—kicking back like they did this every day, knew each other more intimately than they did their husbands or children or boyfriends.

When Dottie Leeds looked up from Shelley's head and said, "Elgin, honey, can we get you a sports page or something?" the whole place burst out laughing, Shelley included. Elgin smiled, though he didn't feel like it, and gave them all a sheepish wave that got a bigger laugh, and he told Shelley he'd be back in a bit and left.

He headed up Main toward the town square, wondering what it was those women seemed to know so effortlessly that completely escaped him, and saw Perkin Lut walking in a circle outside Dexter Isley's Five & Dime. It was one of those days when the wet, white heat was so overpowering that unless you were in Martha's, the one place in town with central air-conditioning, most people stayed inside with their shades down and tried not to move much.

And there was Perkin Lut walking the soles of his shoes into the ground, turning in circles like a little kid trying to make himself dizzy.

Perkin and Elgin had known each other since kindergarten, but Elgin could never remember liking the man much. Perkin's old man, Mance Lut, had pretty much built Eden, and he'd spent a lot of money keeping Perkin out of the war, hid his son up in Chapel Hill, North Carolina, for so many semesters even Perkin couldn't remember what he'd majored in. A lot of men who'd gone overseas and come back hated Perkin for that, as did the families of the men who hadn't come back, but that wasn't Elgin's problem with Perkin. Hell, if Elgin'd had the money, he'd have stayed out of that shitty war too. What Elgin couldn't abide was that there was something in Perkin that not only protected him from consequences but that made him look down on people who paid for their sins, who fell without a safety net to catch them.

It had happened more than once that Elgin had found himself thrusting in and out of Perkin's wife and thinking, Take that, Perkin. Take that.

But this afternoon, Perkin didn't have his salesman's smile or aloof glance. When Elgin stopped by him and said, "Hey, Perkin, how are you?" Perkin looked up at him with eyes so wild they seemed about to jump out of their sockets.

"I'm not good, Elgin. Not good."

"What's the matter?"

Perkin nodded to himself several times, looked over Elgin's shoulder. "I'm fixing to do something about that."

"About what?"

"About that." Perkin's jaw gestured over Elgin's shoulder.

Elgin turned around, looked across Main and through the windows of Miller's Laundromat, saw Jewel Lut pulling her clothes from the dryer, saw Blue standing beside her, taking a pair of jeans from the pile and starting to fold. If either of them had looked up and over they'd have seen Elgin and Perkin Lut easily enough, but Elgin knew they wouldn't. There was an air to the two of them that seemed to block out the rest of the world in that bright Laundromat as easily as it would in a dark bedroom. Blue's lips moved and Jewel laughed, flipped a T-shirt on his head.

"I'm fixing to do something right now," Perkin said.

Elgin looked at him, could see that was a lie, something Perkin was repeating to himself in hopes it would come true. Perkin was successful in business, and for more reasons than just his daddy's money, but he wasn't the kind of man who did things; he was the kind of man who had things done.

Elgin looked across the street again. Blue still had the T-shirt sitting atop his head. He said something else and Jewel covered her mouth with her hand when she laughed.

"Don't you have a washer and dryer at your house, Perkin?"

Perkin rocked back on his heels. "Washer broke. Jewel decides to come in town." He looked at Elgin. "We ain't getting along so well these days. She keeps reading those magazines, Elgin. You know the ones? Talking about liberation, leaving your bra at home, shit like that." He pointed across the street. "Your friend's a problem."

Your friend.

Elgin looked at Perkin, felt a sudden anger he couldn't completely understand, and with it a desire to say, That's my friend and he's talking to my fuck-buddy. Get it, Perkin?

Instead, he just shook his head and left Perkin there, walked across the street to the Laundromat.

Blue took the T-shirt off his head when he saw Elgin enter. A smile, half frozen on his pitted face, died as he blinked into the sunlight blaring through the windows.

Jewel said, "Hey, we got another helper!" She tossed a pair of men's briefs over Blue's head, hit Elgin in the chest with them.

"Hey, Jewel."

"Hey, Elgin. Long time." Her eyes dropped from his, settled on a towel.

Didn't seem like it at the moment to Elgin. Seemed almost as if he'd been out at the lake with her as recently as last night. He could taste her in his mouth, smell her skin damp with a light sweat.

And standing there with Blue, it also seemed like they were all three back in that trailer park, and Jewel hadn't aged a bit. Still wore her red hair long and messy, still dressed in clothes seemed to have been picked up, wrinkled, off her closet floor and nothing fancy about them in the first place, but draped over her body, they were sexier than clothes other rich women bought in New York once a year.

This afternoon, she wore a crinkly, paisley dress that might have been on the pink side once but had faded to a pasty newspaper color after years of washing. Nothing special about it, not too high up her thigh or down her chest, and loose—but something about her body made it appear like she might just ripen right out of it any second.

Elgin handed the briefs to Blue as he joined them at the folding table. For a while, none of them said anything. They picked clothes from the large pile and folded, and the only sound was Jewel whistling.

Then Jewel laughed.

"What?" Blue said.

"Aw, nothing." She shook her head. "Seems like we're just one happy family here, though, don't it?"

Blue looked stunned. He looked at Elgin. He looked at Jewel. He looked at the pair of small, light-blue socks he held in his hands, the monogram *JL* stitched in the cotton. He looked at Jewel again.

"Yeah," he said eventually, and Elgin heard a tremor in his voice he'd never heard before. "Yeah, it does."

Elgin looked up at one of the upper dryer doors. It had swung out at eye level when the dryer had been emptied. The center of the door was a circle of glass, and Elgin could see Main Street reflected in it, the white posts that supported the wood awning over the Five & Dime, Perkin Lut walking in circles, his head down, the heat shimmering in waves up and down Main.

THE DOG WAS green.

Blue had used some of the money Big Bobby'd paid him over the past few weeks to upgrade his target scope. The new scope was huge, twice the width of the rifle barrel, and because the days were getting shorter, it was outfitted with a light-amplification device. Elgin had used similar scopes in the jungle, and he'd never liked them, even when they'd saved his life and those of his platoon, picked up Charlie coming through the dense flora like icy gray ghosts. Night scopes—or LADs as they'd called them over there—were just plain unnatural, and Elgin always felt like he was looking through a telescope from the bottom of a lake. He had no idea where Blue would have gotten one, but hunters in Eden had been showing up with all sorts of weird marine or army surplus shit these last few years; Elgin had even heard of a hunting party using grenades to scare up fish—blowing 'em up into the boat already half cooked, all you had to do was scale 'em.

The dog was green, the highway was beige, the top of the tree line was yellow, and the trunks were the color of army fatigues.

Blue said, "What you think?"

They were up in the tree house Blue'd built. Nice wood, two lawn chairs, a tarp hanging from the branch overhead, a cooler filled with Coors. Blue'd built a railing across the front, perfect for resting your elbows when you took aim. Along the tree trunk, he'd mounted a huge klieg light plugged to a portable generator, because while it was illegal to "shine" deer, nobody'd ever said anything about shining wild dogs. Blue was definitely home.

Elgin shrugged. Just like in the jungle, he wasn't sure he was meant to see the world this way—faded to the shades and textures of old photographs. The dog too seemed to sense that it had stepped out of time somehow, into this seaweed circle punched through the landscape. It sniffed the air with a misshapen snout, but the rest of its body was tensed into one tight muscle, leaning forward as if it smelled prey.

Blue said, "You wanna do it?"

The stock felt hard against Elgin's shoulder. The trigger, curled under his index finger, was cold and thick, something about it that itched his finger and the back of his head simultaneously, a voice back there with the itch in his head saying, "Fire."

What you could never talk about down at the bar to people

who hadn't been there, to people who wanted to know, was what it had been like firing on human beings, on those icy gray ghosts in the dark jungle. Elgin had been in fourteen battles over the course of his twelve-month tour, and he couldn't say with certainty that he'd ever killed anyone. He'd shot some of those shapes, seen them go down, but never the blood, never their eyes when the bullets hit. It had all been a cluster-fuck of swift and sudden noise and color, an explosion of white lights and tracers, green bush, red fire, screams in the night. And afterward, if it was clear, you walked into the jungle and saw the corpses, wondered if you'd hit this body or that one or any at all.

And the only thing you were sure of was that you were too fucking hot and still—this was the terrible thing, but oddly exhilarating too—deeply afraid.

Elgin lowered Blue's rifle, stared across the interstate, now the color of seashell, at the dark mint tree line. The dog was barely noticeable, a soft dark shape amid other soft dark shapes.

He said, "No, Blue, thanks," and handed him the rifle.

Blue said, "Suit yourself, buddy." He reached behind them and pulled the beaded string on the klieg light. As the white light erupted across the highway and the dog froze, blinking in the brightness, Elgin found himself wondering what the fucking point of a LAD scope was when you were just going to shine the animal anyway.

Blue swung the rifle around, leaned into the railing, and put a round in the center of the animal, right by its rib cage. The dog jerked inward, as if someone had whacked it with a bat, and as it teetered on wobbly legs, Blue pulled back on the bolt, drove it home again, and shot the dog in the head. The dog flipped over on its side, most of its skull gone, back leg kicking at the road like it was trying to ride a bicycle.

"You think Jewel Lut might, I dunno, like me?" Blue said.

Elgin cleared his throat. "Sure. She's always liked you."

"But I mean . . ." Blue shrugged, seemed embarrassed suddenly. "How about this: You think a girl like that could take to Australia?"

"Australia?"

Blue smiled at Elgin. "Australia."

"Australia?" he said again.

Blue reached back and shut off the light. "Australia. They got some wild dingoes there, buddy. Could make some real money. Jewel told me the other day how they got real nice beaches. But dingoes too. Big Bobby said people're starting to bitch about what's happening here, asking where Rover is and such, and anyway, ain't too many dogs left dumb enough to come this way anymore. Australia," he said, "they never run out of dog. Sooner or later, here, I'm gonna run out of dog."

Elgin nodded. Sooner or later, Blue would run out of dog. He wondered if Big Bobby'd thought that one through, if he had a contingency plan, if he had access to the National Guard.

"THE BOY'S JUST, what you call it, zealous," Big Bobby told Elgin.

They were sitting in Phil's Barbershop on Main. Phil had gone to lunch, and Big Bobby'd drawn the shades so people'd think he was making some important decision of state.

Elgin said, "He ain't zealous, Big Bobby. He's losing it. Thinks he's in love with Jewel Lut."

"He's always thought that."

"Yeah, but now maybe he's thinking she might like him a bit too."

Big Bobby said, "How come you never call me Mayor?"

Elgin sighed.

"All right, all right. Look," Big Bobby said, picking up one of the hair-tonic bottles on Phil's counter and sniffing it, "so Blue likes his job a little bit."

Elgin said, "There's more to it and you know it."

Playing with combs now. "I do?"

"Bobby, he's got a taste for shooting things now."

"Wait." He held up a pair of fat, stubby hands. "Blue always liked to shoot things. Everyone knows that. Shit, if he wasn't so short and didn't have six or seven million little health problems, he'd a been the first guy in this town to go to The 'Nam. 'Stead, he had to sit back here while you boys had all the fun."

Calling it The 'Nam. Like Big Bobby had any idea. Calling it fun. Shit.

"Dingoes," Elgin said.

"Dingoes?"

"Dingoes. He's saying he's going to Australia to shoot dingoes."

"Do him a world of good too." Big Bobby sat back down in the barber's chair beside Elgin. "He can see the sights, that sort of thing."

"Bobby, he ain't going to Australia and you know it. Hell, Blue ain't never stepped over the county line in his life."

Big Bobby polished his belt buckle with the cuff of his sleeve. "Well, what you want me to do about it?"

"I don't know. I'm just telling you. Next time you see him, Bobby, you look in his fucking eyes."

"Yeah. What'll I see?"

Elgin turned his head, looked at him. "Nothing."

Bobby said, "He's your buddy."

Elgin thought of the small panties curling out of the dust under Blue's bed. "Yeah, but he's your problem."

Big Bobby put his hands behind his head, stretched in the chair. "Well, people getting suspicious about all the dogs disappearing, so I'm going to have to shut this operation down immediately anyway."

He wasn't getting it. "Bobby, you shut this operation down, someone's gonna get a world's worth of that nothing in Blue's eyes."

Big Bobby shrugged, a man who'd made a career out of knowing what was beyond him.

THE FIRST TIME Perkin Lut struck Jewel in public was at Chuck's Diner.

Elgin and Shelley were sitting just three booths away when they heard a racket of falling glasses and plates, and by the time they came out of their booth, Jewel was lying on the tile floor with shattered glass and chunks of bone china by her elbows and Perkin standing over her, his arms shaking, a look in his eyes that said he'd surprised himself as much as anyone else.

Elgin looked at Jewel, on her knees, the hem of her dress getting stained by the spilled food, and he looked away before she caught his eye, because if that happened he just might do something stupid, fuck Perkin up a couple-three ways.

"Aw, Perkin," Chuck Blade said, coming from behind the counter to help Jewel up, wiping gravy off his hands against his apron.

"We don't respect that kind of behavior 'round here, Mr. Lut," Clara Blade said. "Won't have it neither."

Chuck Blade helped Jewel to her feet, his eyes cast down at his broken plates, the half a steak lying in a soup of beans by his shoe. Jewel had a welt growing on her right cheek, turning a bright red as she placed her hand on the table for support.

"I didn't mean it," Perkin said.

Clara Blade snorted and pulled the pen from behind her ear, began itemizing the damage on a cocktail napkin.

"I didn't." Perkin noticed Elgin and Shelley. He locked eyes with Elgin, held out his hands. "I swear."

Elgin turned away and that's when he saw Blue coming through the door. He had no idea where he'd come from, though it ran through his head that Blue could have just been standing outside looking in, could have been standing there for an hour.

Like a lot of small guys, Blue had speed, and he never seemed to walk in a straight line. He moved as if he were constantly sidestepping tackles or land mines—with sudden, unpredictable pivots that left you watching the space where he'd been, instead of the place he'd ended up.

Blue didn't say anything, but Elgin could see the homicide in his eyes and Perkin saw it too, backed up, and slipped on the mess on the floor and stumbled back, trying to regain his balance as Blue came past Shelley and tried to lunge past Elgin.

Elgin caught him at the waist, lifted him off the ground, and held on tight because he knew how slippery Blue could be in these situations. You'd think you had him and he'd just squirm away from you, hit somebody with a glass.

Elgin tucked his head down and headed for the door, Blue flopped over his shoulder like a bag of cement mix, Blue screaming, "You see me, Perkin? You see me? I'm a last face you see, Perkin! Real soon."

Elgin hit the open doorway, felt the night heat on his face as Blue screamed, "Jewel! You all right? Jewel?"

BLUE DIDN'T SAY much back at Elgin's trailer.

He tried to explain to Shelley how pure Jewel was, how hitting something that innocent was like spitting on the Bible.

Shelley didn't say anything, and after a while Blue shut up too.

Elgin just kept plying him with Beam, knowing Blue's lack of tolerance for it, and pretty soon Blue passed out on the couch, his pitted face still red with rage.

"HE'S NEVER BEEN exactly right in the head, has he?" Shelley said.

Elgin ran his hand down her bare arm, pulled her shoulder in tighter against his chest, heard Blue snoring from the front of the trailer. "No, ma'am."

She rose above him, her dark hair falling to his face, tickling the corners of his eyes. "But you've been his friend."

Elgin nodded.

She touched his cheek with her hand. "Why?"

Elgin thought about it a bit, started talking to her about the little, dirty kid and his cockroach flambés, of the animal sounds that came from his mother's trailer. The way Blue used to sit by the drainage ditch, all pulled into himself, his body tight. Elgin thought of all those roaches and cats and rabbits and dogs, and he told Shelley that he'd always thought Blue was dying, ever since he'd met him, leaking away in front of his eyes.

"Everyone dies," she said.

"Yeah." He rose up on his elbow, rested his free hand on her warm hip. "Yeah, but with most of us it's like we're growing toward something and then we die. But with Blue, it's like he ain't never grown toward nothing. He's just been dying real slowly since he was born."

She shook her head. "I'm not getting you."

He thought of the mildew that used to soak the walls in Blue's mother's trailer, of the mold and dust in Blue's shack off Route 11, of the rotting smell that had grown out of the drainage ditch when they were kids. The way Blue looked at it all—seemed to be at one with it—as if he felt a bond.

Shelley said, "Babe, what do you think about getting out of here?"

"Where?"

"I dunno. Florida. Georgia. Someplace else."

"I got a job. You too."

"You can always get construction jobs other places. Reception-ist jobs too."

"We grew up here."

She nodded. "But maybe it's time to start our life somewhere else."

He said, "Let me think about it."

She tilted his chin so she was looking in his eyes. "You've *been* thinking about it."

He nodded. "Maybe I want to think about it some more."

IN THE MORNING, when they woke up, Blue was gone.

Shelley looked at the rumpled couch, over at Elgin. For a good minute they just stood there, looking from the couch to each other, the couch to each other.

An hour later, Shelley called from work, told Elgin that Perkin Lut was in his office as always, no signs of physical damage.

Elgin said, "If you see Blue . . ."

"Yeah?"

Elgin thought about it. "I dunno. Call the cops. Tell Perkin to bail out a back door. That sound right?"

"Sure."

BIG BOBBY CAME to the site later that morning, said, "I go over to Blue's place to tell him we got to end this dog thing and—"

"Did you tell him it was over?" Elgin asked.

"Let me finish. Let me explain."

"Did you tell him?"

"Let me finish." Bobby wiped his face with a handkerchief. "I was gonna tell him, but—"

"You didn't tell him."

"But Jewel Lut was there."

"What?"

Big Bobby put his hand on Elgin's elbow, led him away from the other workers. "I said Jewel was there. The two of them sitting at the kitchen table, having breakfast."

"In Blue's place?"

Big Bobby nodded. "Biggest dump I ever seen. Smells like something I-don't-know-what. But bad. And there's Jewel, pretty as can be in her summer dress and soft skin and makeup, eating Eggos and grits with Blue, big brown shiner under her eye. She smiles at me, says, 'Hey, Big Bobby,' and goes back to eating."

"And that was it?"

"How come no one ever calls me Mayor?"

"And that was it?" Elgin repeated.

"Yeah. Blue asks me to take a seat, I say I got business. He says him too."

"What's that mean?" Elgin heard his own voice, hard and sharp.

Big Bobby took a step back from it. "Hell do I know? Could mean he's going out to shoot more dog."

"So you never told him you were shutting down the operation."

Big Bobby's eyes were wide and confused. "You hear what I told

you? He was in there with Jewel. Her all doll-pretty and him looking, well, ugly as usual. Whole situation was too weird. I got out."

"Blue said he had business too."

"He said he had business too," Bobby said, and walked away.

THE NEXT WEEK, they showed up in town together a couple of
times, buying some groceries, toiletries for Jewel, boxes of shells for
Blue.

They never held hands or kissed or did anything romantic, but
they were together, and people talked. Said, Well, of all things. And
I never thought I'd see the day. How do you like that? I guess this
is the day the cows actually come home.

Blue called and invited Shelley and Elgin to join them one Sunday afternoon for a late breakfast at the IHOP. Shelley begged off,
said something about coming down with the flu, but Elgin went.
He was curious to see where this was going, what Jewel was thinking, how she thought her hanging around Blue was going to come
to anything but bad.

He could feel the eyes of the whole place on them as they ate.

"See where he hit me?" Jewel tilted her head, tucked her beautiful red hair back behind her ear. The mark on her cheekbone, in
the shape of a small rain puddle, was faded yellow now, its edges
roped by a sallow beige.

Elgin nodded.

"Still can't believe the son of a bitch hit me," she said, but there
was no rage in her voice anymore, just a mild sense of drama, as if
she'd pushed the words out of her mouth the way she believed she

should say them. But the emotion she must have felt when Perkin's hand hit her face, when she fell to the floor in front of people she'd known all her life—that seemed to have faded with the mark on her cheekbone.

"Perkin Lut," she said with a snort, then laughed.

Elgin looked at Blue. He'd never seemed so . . . fluid in all the time Elgin had known him. The way he cut into his pancakes, swept them off his plate with a smooth dip of the fork tines; the swift dab of the napkin against his lips after every bite; the attentive swivel of his head whenever Jewel spoke, usually in tandem with the lifting of his coffee mug to his mouth.

This was not a Blue Elgin recognized. Except when he was handling weapons, Blue moved in jerks and spasms. Tremors rippled through his limbs and caused his fingers to drop things, his elbows and knees to move too fast, crack against solid objects. Blue's blood seemed to move too quickly through his veins, made his muscles obey his brain after a quarter-second delay and then too rapidly, as if to catch up on lost time.

But now he moved in concert, like an athlete or a jungle cat.

That's what you do to men, Jewel: You give them a confidence so total it finds their limbs.

"Perkin," Blue said, and rolled his eyes at Jewel and they both laughed.

She not as hard as he did, though.

Elgin could see the root of doubt in her eyes, could feel her loneliness in the way she fiddled with the menu, touched her cheekbone, spoke too loudly, as if she wasn't just telling Elgin and Blue how Perkin had mistreated her, but the whole IHOP as well, so people could get it straight that she wasn't the villain, and if after she returned to Perkin she had to leave him again, they'd know why.

Of course she was going back to Perkin.

Elgin could tell by the glances she gave Blue—unsure, slightly embarrassed, maybe a bit repulsed. What had begun as a nighttime ride into the unknown had turned cold and stale during the hard yellow lurch into morning.

Blue wiped his mouth, said, "Be right back," and walked to the bathroom with surer strides than Elgin had ever seen on the man.

Elgin looked at Jewel.

She gripped the handle of her coffee cup between the tips of her thumb and index finger and turned the cup in slow revolutions around the saucer, made a soft scraping noise that climbed up Elgin's spine like a termite trapped under the skin.

"You ain't sleeping with him, are you?" Elgin said quietly.

Jewel's head jerked up and she looked over her shoulder, then back at Elgin. "What? God, no. We're just . . . He's my pal. That's all. Like when we were kids."

"We ain't kids."

"I know. Don't you think I know?" She fingered the coffee cup again. "I miss you," she said softly. "I miss you. When you coming back?"

Elgin kept his voice low. "Me and Shelley, we're getting pretty serious."

She gave him a small smile that he instantly hated. It seemed to know him; it seemed like everything he was and everything he wasn't was caught in the curl of her lips. "You miss the lake, Elgin. Don't lie."

He shrugged.

"You ain't ever going to marry Shelley Briggs, have babies, be an upstanding citizen."

"Yeah? Why's that?"

"Because you got too many demons in you, boy. And they need me. They need the lake. They need to cry out every now and then."

Elgin looked down at his own coffee cup. "You going back to Perkin?"

She shook her head hard. "No way. Uh-uh. No way."

Elgin nodded, even though he knew she was lying. If Elgin's demons needed the lake, needed to be unbridled, Jewel's needed Perkin. They needed security. They needed to know the money'd never run out, that she'd never go two full days without a solid meal like she had so many times as a child in the trailer park.

Perkin was what she saw when she looked down at her empty coffee cup, when she touched her cheek. Perkin was at their nice home with his feet up, watching a game, petting the dog, and she was in the IHOP in the middle of a Sunday when the food was at its oldest and coldest, with one guy who loved her and one who fucked her, wondering how she got there.

Blue came back to the table, moving with that new sure stride, a broad smile in the wide swing of his arms.

"How we doing?" Blue said. "Huh? How we doing?" And his lips burst into a grin so huge Elgin expected it to keep going right off the sides of his face.

JEWEL LEFT BLUE'S place two days later, walked into Perkin Lut's Auto Emporium and into Perkin's office, and by the time anyone went to check, they'd left through the back door, gone home for the day.

Elgin tried to get ahold of Blue for three days—called constantly, went by his shack and knocked on the door, even staked out the tree house along I-95 where he fired on the dogs.

He'd decided to break into Blue's place, was fixing to do just that, when he tried one last call from his trailer that third night and Blue answered with a strangled "Hello."

"It's me. How you doing?"

"Can't talk now."

"Come on, Blue. It's me. You okay?"

"All alone," Blue said.

"I know. I'll come by."

"You do, I'll leave."

"Blue."

"Leave me alone for a spell, Elgin. Okay?"

THAT NIGHT ELGIN sat alone in his trailer, smoking cigarettes, staring at the walls.

Blue'd never had much of anything his whole life—not a job he enjoyed, not a woman he could consider his—and then between the dogs and Jewel Lut he'd probably thought he'd got it all at once. Hit pay dirt.

Elgin remembered the dirty little kid sitting down by the drainage ditch, hugging himself. Six, maybe seven years old, waiting to die.

You had to wonder sometimes why some people were even

born. You had to wonder what kind of creature threw bodies into the world, expected them to get along when they'd been given no tools, no capacity to get any either.

In Vietnam, this fat boy, name of Woodson from South Dakota, had been the least popular guy in the platoon. He wasn't smart, he wasn't athletic, he wasn't funny, he wasn't even personable. He just was. Elgin had been running beside him one day through a sea of rice paddies, their boots making sucking sounds every step they took, and someone fired a hell of a round from the other side of the paddies, ripped Woodson's head in half so completely all Elgin saw running beside him for a few seconds was the lower half of Woodson's face. No hair, no forehead, no eyes. Just half the nose, a mouth, a chin.

Thing was, Woodson kept running, kept plunging his feet in and out of the water, making those sucking sounds, M-16 hugged to his chest, for a good eight or ten steps. Kid was dead, he's still running. Kid had no reason to hold on, but he don't know it, he keeps running.

What spark of memory, hope, or dream had kept him going?

You had to wonder.

IN ELGIN'S DREAM that night, a platoon of ice-gray Vietcong rose in a straight line from the center of Cooper's Lake while Elgin was inside the cabin with Shelley and Jewel. He penetrated them both somehow, their separate torsos branching out from the same pair of hips, their four legs clamping at the small of his back, this Shelley-Jewel creature crying out for more, more, more.

And Elgin could see the VC platoon drifting in formation toward the shore, their guns pointed, their faces hidden behind thin wisps of green fog.

The Shelley-Jewel creature arched her backs on the bed below him, and Woodson and Blue stood in the corner of the room, watching as their dogs padded across the floor, letting out low growls and drooling.

Shelley dissolved into Jewel as the VC platoon reached the porch steps and released their safeties all at once, the sound like the ratcheting of a thousand shotguns. Sweat exploded in Elgin's hair, poured down his body like warm rain, and the VC fired in concert, the bullets shearing the walls of the cabin, lifting the roof off into the night. Elgin looked above him at the naked night sky, the stars zipping by like tracers, the yellow moon full and mean, the shivering branches of birch trees. Jewel rose and straddled him, bit his lip, and dug her nails into his back, and the bullets danced through his hair, and then Jewel was gone, her writhing flesh having dissolved into his own.

Elgin sat naked on the bed, his arms stretched wide, waiting for the bullets to find his back, to shear his head from his body the way they'd sheared the roof from the cabin, and the yellow moon burned above him as the dogs howled and Blue and Woodson held each other in the corner of the room and wept like children as the bullets drilled holes in their faces.

BIG BOBBY CAME by the trailer late the next morning, a Sunday, and said, "Blue's a bit put out about losing his job."

"What?" Elgin sat on the edge of his bed, pulled on his socks. "You picked now—now, Bobby—to fire him?"

"It's in his eyes," Big Bobby said. "Like you said. You can see it."

Elgin had seen Big Bobby scared before, plenty of times, but now the man was trembling.

Elgin said, "Where is he?"

BLUE'S FRONT DOOR was open, hanging half down the steps from a busted hinge. Elgin said, "Blue."

"Kitchen."

He sat in his Jockeys at the table, cleaning his rifle, each shiny black piece spread in front of him on the table. Elgin's eyes watered a bit because there was a stench coming from the back of the house that he felt might strip his nostrils bare. He realized then that he'd never asked Big Bobby or Blue what they'd done with all those dead dogs.

Blue said, "Have a seat, bud. Beer in the fridge if you're thirsty."

Elgin wasn't looking in that fridge. "Lost your job, huh?"

Blue wiped the bolt with a shammy cloth. "Happens." He looked at Elgin. "Where you been lately?"

"I called you last night."

"I mean in general."

"Working."

"No, I mean at night."

"Blue, you been"—he almost said "playing house with Jewel Lut" but caught himself—"up in a fucking tree, how do you know where I been at night?"

"I don't," Blue said. "Why I'm asking."

Elgin said, "I've been at my trailer or down at Doubles, same as usual."

"With Shelley Briggs, right?"

Slowly, Elgin said, "Yeah."

"I'm just asking, buddy. I mean, when we all going to go out? You, me, your new girl."

The pits that covered Blue's face like a layer of bad meat had faded some from all those nights in the tree.

Elgin said, "Anytime you want."

Blue put down the bolt. "How 'bout right now?" He stood and walked into the bedroom just off the kitchen. "Let me just throw on some duds."

"She's working now, Blue."

"At Perkin Lut's? Hell, it's almost noon. I'll talk to Perkin about that Dodge he sold me last year, and when she's ready we'll take her out someplace nice." He came back into the kitchen wearing a soiled brown T-shirt and jeans.

"Hell," Elgin said, "I don't want the girl thinking I've got some serious love for her or something. We come by for lunch, next thing she'll expect me to drop her off in the mornings, pick her up at night."

Blue was reassembling the rifle, snapping all those shiny pieces together so fast Elgin figured he could do it blind. He said, "Elgin, you got to show them some affection sometimes. I mean, Jesus." He pulled a thin brass bullet from his T-shirt pocket and slipped it in the breech, followed it with four more, then slid the bolt home.

"Yeah, but you know what I'm saying, bud?" Elgin watched

Blue nestle the stock in the space between his left hip and ribs, let the barrel point out into the kitchen.

"I know what you're saying," Blue said. "I know. But I got to talk to Perkin about my Dodge."

"What's wrong with it?"

"What's wrong with it?" Blue turned to look at him, and the barrel swung level with Elgin's belt buckle. "What's wrong with it, it's a piece of shit, what's wrong with it, Elgin. Hell, you know that. Perkin sold me a lemon. This is the situation." He blinked. "Beer for the ride?"

Elgin had a pistol in his glove compartment. A .32. He considered it.

"Elgin?"

"Yeah?"

"Why you looking at me funny?"

"You got a rifle pointed at me, Blue. You realize that?"

Blue looked at the rifle, and its presence seemed to surprise him. He dipped it toward the floor. "Shit, man, I'm sorry. I wasn't even thinking. It feels like my arm sometimes. I forget. Man, I am sorry." He held his arms out wide, the rifle rising with them.

"Lotta things deserve to die, don't they?"

Blue smiled. "Well, I wasn't quite thinking along those lines, but now you bring it up . . ."

Elgin said, "Who deserves to die, buddy?"

Blue laughed. "You got something on your mind, don't you?" He hoisted himself up on the table, cradled the rifle in his lap. "Hell, boy, who you got? Let's start with people who take two parking spaces."

"Okay." Elgin moved the chair by the table to a position slightly behind Blue, sat in it. "Let's."

"Then there's DJs talk through the first minute of a song. Fucking Guatos coming down here these days to pick tobacco, showing no respect. Women wearing all those tight clothes, look at you like you're a pervert when you stare at what they're advertising." He wiped his forehead with his arm. "Shit."

"Who else?" Elgin said quietly.

"Okay. Okay. You got people like the ones let their dogs run wild into the highway, get themselves killed. And you got dishonest people, people who lie and sell insurance and cars and bad food. You got a lot of things. Jane Fonda."

"Sure." Elgin nodded.

Blue's face was drawn, gray. He crossed his legs over each other like he used to down at the drainage ditch. "It's all out there." He nodded and his eyelids drooped.

"Perkin Lut?" Elgin said. "He deserve to die?"

"Not just Perkin," Blue said. "Not just. Lots of people. I mean, how many you kill over in the war?"

Elgin shrugged. "I don't know."

"But some. Some. Right? Had to. I mean, that's war—someone gets on your bad side, you kill them and all their friends till they stop bothering you." His eyelids drooped again, and he yawned so deeply he shuddered when he finished.

"Maybe you should get some sleep."

Blue looked over his shoulder at him. "You think? It's been a while."

A breeze rattled the thin walls at the back of the house, pushed that thick dank smell into the kitchen again, a rotting stench that found the back of Elgin's throat and stuck there. He said, "When's the last time?"

"I slept? Hell, a while. Days maybe." Blue twisted his body so he was facing Elgin. "You ever feel like you spend your whole life waiting for it to get going?"

Elgin nodded, not positive what Blue was saying, but knowing he should agree with him. "Sure."

"It's hard," Blue said. "Hard." He leaned back on the table, stared at the brown water marks in his ceiling.

Elgin took in a long stream of that stench through his nostrils. He kept his eyes open, felt that air entering his nostrils creep past into his corneas, tear at them. The urge to close his eyes and wish it all away was as strong an urge as he'd ever felt, but he knew now was that time he'd always known was coming.

He leaned in toward Blue, reached across him, and pulled the rifle off his lap.

Blue turned his head, looked at him.

"Go to sleep," Elgin said. "I'll take care of this a while. We'll go see Shelley tomorrow. Perkin Lut too."

Blue blinked. "What if I can't sleep? Huh? I've been having that problem, you know. I put my head on the pillow and I try to sleep and it won't come and soon I'm just bawling like a fucking child till I got to get up and do something."

Elgin looked at the tears that had sprung into Blue's eyes, the red veins split across the whites, the desperate, savage need in his face that had always been there if anyone had looked close enough, and would never, Elgin knew, be satisfied.

"I'll stick right here, buddy. I'll sit here in the kitchen and you go in and sleep."

Blue turned his head and stared up at the ceiling again. Then he slid off the table, peeled off his T-shirt, and tossed it on top of the fridge. "All right. All right. I'm gonna try." He stopped at the bedroom doorway. " 'Member—there's beer in the fridge. You be here when I wake up?"

Elgin looked at him. He was still so small, probably so thin you could still wrap your hand around his biceps, meet the fingers on the other side. He was still ugly and stupid-looking, still dying right in front of Elgin's eyes.

"I'll be here, Blue. Don't you worry."

"Good enough. Yes, sir."

Blue shut the door and Elgin heard the bedsprings grind, the rustle of pillows being arranged. He sat in the chair, with the smell of whatever decayed in the back of the house swirling around his head. The sun had hit the cheap tin roof now, and after a while he realized the buzzing he'd thought was in his head came from somewhere back in the house too.

He wondered if he had the strength to open the fridge. He wondered if he should call Perkin Lut's and tell Perkin to get the hell out of Eden for a bit. Maybe he'd just ask for Shelley, tell her to meet him tonight with her suitcases. They'd drive down 95 where the dogs wouldn't disturb them, drive clear to Jacksonville, Florida, before the sun came up again. See if they could outrun Blue and his tiny, dangerous wants, his dog corpses, and his smell; outrun people who took two parking spaces and telephone solicitors and Jane Fonda.

Jewel flashed through his mind then, an image of her sitting atop him, arching her back and shaking that long red hair, a look in her green eyes that said this was it, this was why we live.

He could stand up right now with this rifle in his hands, scratch the itch in the back of his head, and fire straight through the door, end what should never have been started.

He sat there staring at the door for quite a while, until he knew the exact number of places the paint had peeled in teardrop spots, and eventually he stood, went to the phone on the wall by the fridge, and dialed Perkin Lut's.

"Auto Emporium," Shelley said, and Elgin thanked God that in his present mood he hadn't gotten Glynnis Verdon, who snapped her gum and always placed him on hold, left him listening to Muzak versions of the Shirelles.

"Shelley?"

"People gonna talk, you keep calling me at work, boy."

He smiled, cradled the rifle like a baby, leaned against the wall. "How you doing?"

"Just fine, handsome. How 'bout yourself?"

Elgin turned his head, looked at the bedroom door. "I'm okay."

"Still like me?"

Elgin heard the springs creak in the bedroom, heard weight drop on the old floorboards. "Still like you."

"Well, then, it's all fine then, isn't it?"

Blue's footfalls crossed toward the bedroom door, and Elgin used his hip to push himself off the wall.

"It's all fine," he said. "I gotta go. I'll talk to you soon."

He hung up and stepped away from the wall.

"Elgin," Blue said from the other side of the door.

"Yeah, Blue?"

"I can't sleep. I just can't."

Elgin saw Woodson sloshing through the paddy, the top of his head gone. He saw the pink panties curling up from underneath Blue's bed and a shaft of sunlight hitting Shelley's face as she looked up from behind her desk at Perkin Lut's and smiled. He saw Jewel Lut dancing in the night rain by the lake and that dog lying dead on the shoulder of the interstate, kicking its leg like it was trying to ride a bicycle.

"Elgin," Blue said. "I just can't sleep. I got to do something."

"Try," Elgin said and cleared his throat.

"I just can't. I got to . . . do something. I got to go . . ." His voice cracked, and he cleared his throat. "I can't sleep."

The doorknob turned and Elgin raised the rifle, stared down the barrel.

"Sure, you can, Blue." He curled his finger around the trigger as the door opened. "Sure you can," he repeated and took a breath, held it in.

THE SKELETON OF Eden Falls still sits on twenty-two acres of land just east of Brimmer's Point, covered in rust thick as flesh. Some say it was the levels of iodine an environmental inspector found in the groundwater that scared off the original investors. Others said it was the downswing of the state economy or the governor's failed reelection bid. Some say Eden Falls was just plain a dumb name, too biblical. And then, of course, there were plenty who claimed it was Jewel Lut's ghost scared off all the workers.

They found her body hanging from the scaffolding they'd erected by the shell of the roller coaster. She was naked and hung upside down from a rope tied around her ankles. Her throat had been cut so deep the coroner said it was a miracle her head was still attached when they found her. The coroner's assistant, man by the name of Chris Gleason, would claim when he was in his cups that the head had fallen off in the hearse as they drove down Main toward the morgue. Said he heard it cry out.

This was the same day Elgin Bern called the sheriff's office, told them he'd shot his buddy Blue, fired two rounds into him at close range, the little guy dead before he hit his kitchen floor. Elgin told the deputy he was still sitting in the kitchen, right where he'd done it a few hours before. Said to send the hearse.

Due to the fact that Perkin Lut had no real alibi for his whereabouts when Jewel passed on and owing to the fact there'd been some very recent and very public discord in their marriage, Perkin was arrested and brought before a grand jury, but that jury decided not to indict. Perkin and Jewel had been patching things up, after all; he'd bought her a car (at cost, but still . . .).

Besides, we all knew it was Blue had killed Jewel. Hell, the Simmons boy, a retard ate paint and tree bark, could have told you that. Once all that stuff came out about what Blue and Big Bobby'd been doing with the dogs around here, well, that just sealed it. And everyone remembered how that week she'd been separated from Perkin, you could see the dream come alive in Blue's eyes, see him allow hope into his heart for the first time in his sorry life.

And when hope comes late to a man, it's a dangerous thing. Hope is for the young, the children. Hope in a full-grown man—particularly one with as little acquaintanceship with it or prospect for it as Blue—well, that kind of hope burns as it dies, boils blood white, and leaves something mean behind when it's done.

Blue killed Jewel Lut.

And Elgin Bern killed Blue. And ended up doing time. Not much, due to his war record and the circumstances of who Blue was, but time just the same. Everyone knew Blue probably had it coming, was probably on his way back into town to do to Perkin or some other poor soul what he'd done to Jewel. Once a man gets that look in his eyes—that boiled look, like a dog searching out a bone who's not going to stop until he finds it— well, sometimes he has to be put down like a dog. Don't he?

And it was sad how Elgin came out of prison to find Shelley Briggs gone, moved up North with Perkin Lut of all people, who'd lost his heart for the car business after Jewel died, took to selling home electronics imported from Japan and Germany, made himself a fortune. Not long after he got out of prison, El-gin left too, no one knows where, just gone, drifting.

See, the thing is—no one wanted to convict Elgin. We all understood. We did. Blue had to go. But he'd had no weapon in his hand when Elgin, standing just nine feet away, pulled that trigger. Twice. Once we might have been able to overlook,

but twice, that's something else again. Elgin offered no de-
fense, even refused a fancy lawyer's attempt to get him to claim
he'd suffered something called Post-Traumatic Stress Disorder,
which we're hearing a lot more about these days.

"I don't have that," Elgin said. "I shot a defenseless man.
That's the long and the short of it, and that's a sin."

And he was right:

In the world, 'case you haven't noticed, you usually pay for
your sins.

And in the South, always.

ICU

THIS WOMAN, CARRIE, regular in the bar, she says to him, "There was a guy around asking about you."

Daniel turns on his stool. He catches the reflection of one of his eyebrows in her iris, and it bothers him, makes him feel as if it's trapped in there and she might not give it back.

He says, "What guy?"

She shrugs, taking his eyebrow with her as she turns back to her vodka-n-whatever. "Some guy. He was in earlier. Wore a tie and everything. I asked him if he sold cars."

"Did he?"

"He said no, but guys, you know? Lie about a fucking hangover they're puking in the sink. This guy once, right? Calls me Doreen, okay? Doreen. Shit . . ."

She rattles her ice cubes. She takes a hit off her cigarette.

He waits for more but she juts her head forward and bulges her eyes to get the bartender's attention.

He says, "So this guy who didn't sell cars . . ."

She nods several times, quick, but she's nodding at the bartender and she says, " 'Nother, hon', thanks." She turns toward him, blowing smoke. "Your name's Donnie, right?"

"Daniel."

"Danny, I got to tell you, this guy? He said I should stay the fuck away from you."

He doesn't know how to respond to this. He's never bothered this woman. Barely spoken to her. She's a regular, he's a regular. He's bought her a drink or two. (Once, yeah, back in December when they were the only two in the place the entire night, he bought her four and danced with her once, the jukebox playing "You Got My Sugar but I Got You, Sweet" as the snow fell like cotton swabs outside the high green windows. Then the bartender said closing time and Daniel asked her if she was okay to drive and she laughed and the sound of it was like a bird screeching above the ocean and she slapped both hands on his chest and said, "Yeah, I'm fine, sweetie. You go on home.")

He says, "Why?"

"Why what?" Lifting her drink to toast the bartender for bringing it.

"Why stay the fuck away?"

She shrugs. "I dunno. But he meant it."

"But you never met him before."

"So?"

"So why trust his opinion?"

She looks at him.

It's his nose in her iris this time, the tip of it, bobbing.

"Tim," she calls.

Tim is the bartender. He makes his way over, leans his elbow by her glass, eyebrows up. Tim likes no one. Tim has a single red tattoo on his right forearm. It's covered in hair and faded. A flower with a broken stem and the word *good-bye* underneath it. Tim is the kind of guy Daniel doesn't understand with awe.

Tim says, "What?"

Carrie says, "This guy's bothering me."

HE GOES TO one of his other bars. He tries to tell the bartender about Carrie, her crazy story, her getting him ejected, but the bartender's got glasses to wipe.

It's a younger crowd in here, noisier, but he finds a corner seat and watches the TVs. Basketball on one, bombs on the others. Roofs and streets of the ancient city lit up like a thousand tongues, licking the sky, afire. A yellow ticker running below it all that Daniel finds gorgeous and absurd. The world needs a yellow ticker, he is pretty sure. Just to keep score. Just to rid it of things of the nonticker variety. She was here . . . CNN . . . She's not . . . FOX NEWS . . . Two kids . . . CSPAN . . . Die alone . . . MSNBC . . .

A guy he knows, gin-n-tonic-hates-his-job-curly-amber-hair sits beside him and sighs. "Time was you didn't have to wait for a toilet in this place."

Daniel says, "Saturdays."

"Time was . . . ," the guy says.

On the TV, something blows up, breathless and huge.

"Time was . . . ," the guy says.

Guy's got two feet of bar in front of him, he keeps missing it with his elbow. His hair is dark with sweat.

Daniel stares up at the TV, wondering if the guy will face-plant.

Another tongue goes afire. A man with a microphone and a beige safari jacket with a shitload of pockets blocks the flaming tongue. He looks somber. Respectful.

Daniel wonders where they sell those jackets.

Guy beside him snores.

Bartender leans in and says, "Two guys in here earlier?"

"Yeah?"

Bartender turns his chin, yawns into his fist. He reaches down for a bottle of peach schnapps. "Looking for you."

"What?"

Bartender looks at him. "Wore ties and everything."

DANIEL'S BOSS SAYS, "Now don't cry."

Daniel says, "I'm not crying."

"Well, you are."

"I'm sorry."

His boss says, "*I'm* sorry. Jesus Christ. It's just, you know, the times. It's just, you know, the fucking economy. Your COBRA, though? That's good another, like, nine months."

Daniel says, "I've worked here for—"

"Don't, all right?" His boss hands a box of tissues across the desk.

"THEY CAME TO the house," his ex-wife says.

"When?"

His ex-wife says, "I can't let the boys go with you."

He says, "What?"

His ex-wife says, "I just can't. They asked all these questions."

His ex-wife looks at him, love or pity trapped behind her skin, her bones, those eyes.

"They?"

Love, he thinks. Today, we'll say it's love.

She nods. "There were three of them."

THE MAN APPROACHES Daniel in the express self-checkout aisle. Daniel runs a container of half-and-half over the red laser-light scanner and watches the price appear on the screen in front of him. He's just realized that a sudden-impulse *People* buy tips the total of his items to thirteen, one over the limit, and he hopes that the scanner won't sound an alarm, cancel the whole transaction, alert the management, the line of customers behind him. He looks over his shoulder and the man is standing next to him. Wool scarf over a suede jacket and a dark polo shirt. Lean. A sweep of brown hair hanging over his forehead, so perfectly sharp you could crease a sheet with it.

"How you doing?" the man says.

"Fine." Daniel waves a box of Rice-A-Roni over the red beam.

"Hell of a news day," the man says.

"Yeah?" Daniel tries to look distracted by his open plastic bag in its metal bin.

"Oh, sure."

Daniel places a head of lettuce on the scanner. He faces the screen and selects "produce." He enters "lettuce" on the screen that follows that one. The price appears in bold and is added to his subtotal.

"Seems a high price," the man says.

Daniel scans a half gallon of skim milk.

"For lettuce," the man says.

IN THE PARKING lot, the man right behind him, Daniel wonders if he should walk to his own car or loiter by someone else's.

The guy says, "Daniel."

Daniel stops, looks back at the man with his nice clothes, his L.A.-white teeth, his lack of groceries.

The man puts his hands in his pockets and leans back on his heels. Daniel can't think of anything to say. The man's eyes are the clear and the bright of skyscraper panes.

The man looks down at his shoes and gives them a small smile, as if surprised they still cover his feet, as if conferring with them about how they got there.

He looks back at Daniel, and the small smile holds.

The man says, "That's your car, right?"

A woman pushes her shopping cart past them, wheels scraping the loose cement. A small boy walks a few steps behind her, talking to his action figure, tugging its head to see what will happen.

Daniel waits for the man's eyes to change.

The man jingles the change in his pockets and raises his eyebrows up and down.

Daniel says, "I don't know why you're—"

The man takes a step toward him. Then one more. He looks into Daniel. He says, "You want it to be one way. I understand. I do. But it's the other way."

Daniel feels a small vibration below his Adam's apple, as if a beetle, nestled in the hollow of his throat all winter, is waking up.

Daniel says, "I just want—"

The man shakes his head. "It's the other way."

He says, "I just want everything to go back to—"

"Ssshh," the man says.

The man says, "Daniel."

The man says, "Knock-knock."

Daniel says, "Who's there?"

The man gives him another smile, slightly broader, and leaves the parking lot.

HE DECIDES TO name the man Troy. He seems like a Troy. Logical, smooth-haired, stainless.

He sees Troy outside a bar one night. He's across the street, leaning against a wall and eating what could be yogurt, using a plastic spoon. Another time, he's at the mall, where Daniel has gone to wander, to feel other people, hear piped-in music no matter how bad, if only because he hasn't programmed it himself. He finds something comforting in this, a freedom in the freedom from decision similar to when he comes across a movie on TV, mid-story, and it's a movie he owns on DVD, one he could easily play on the TV himself, without commercials, and with the added advantage of being able to pause for bathroom breaks and beer runs. And yet he doesn't insert the DVD into the player. He doesn't opt for control.

And so the mall speakers play "Lady in Red." They play "Ob-la-di, Ob-la-da." They play Céline Dion and Dave Matthews and Elton John and Mariah Carey. And Daniel, who likes only one of those songs, feels buffeted.

Troy passes him and stops to smile at something in the window of the Payless shoe store. As if the loafers are particularly amusing. As if, through glass, they tell him jokes.

HIS EX-WIFE SAYS to him on the phone, "I'm sorry you're going through this. You're a nice guy."

"I am?"

"You are."

He says, "Would you tell them that?"

She says, "They don't listen. They'll never—"

The phone dies.

Nothing sinister.

Batteries.

HE DRIVES OUT to interview for a job. He does this every day. Always with a blue Toyota Sequoia four or five cars back in traffic.

He would have expected something boxier, brown, low-to-the-ground, American. No. A big-ass, bright blue SUV. With fog lights.

Sometimes they pass him. Just for shits-n-giggles, he supposes. Always back behind him when he reaches wherever he'll interview. For jobs he never gets.

This morning, he's in the medical district. Six hospitals in a seven-block area, connected by breezeways, connected by parking lots, a food court in the center of the tallest building so the anxious and the grieving and the doctors and the bedpan-cleaners can eat Sbarro, Au Bon Pain, Panda Express, Dunkin' Donuts.

That's where he's going—the Dunkin' Donuts. That's what he's been reduced to. The economy, you know. A college graduate (not much of a college, true, but just the same . . .) with fifteen solid years of work experience. And this is the sum total of his life. Interviewing for an assistant manager's position. At a doughnut shop. Nearing forty.

At best, if all returns to normalcy, he will still be alone.

As he pulls into one of the garages on the eastern edge of the seven-block perimeter, a beige Volvo pulls up behind him, and then the lumpy Sequoia noses up behind the Volvo.

He takes his ticket. He pulls forward. The yellow gate-arm goes down behind his car, and he sees in his rearview as the driver of the Volvo reaches for her ticket from the machine and drops it. He watches the ticket fall to the ground and then a tuft of wind flicks it under the car. The woman gets out of her car. She seems confused as to where the ticket went.

Daniel feels a flapping in his chest, an odd and startled faith. He watches the woman peer at the ground like it contained cave drawings, sees the Sequoia trapped behind her, and he puts his car in gear and drives up the ramp.

He turns with the curve of the ramp, and he sees Troy's smile and his wife's trapped pity, and he sees his mother who died in this same hospital complex surrounded by beeps and blips and a TV hung above her that was void of sound but primed with image, and he fishtails coming out of the first turn and those wings flap harder.

He reaches the second floor and cuts the wheels hard and passes a DO NOT ENTER sign and drives up the exit ramp. It's a blind curve, and he envisions the grille of another car appearing before him as if through water, and he wishes he were going fast enough for the risk of fatality to lie in the risk of collision. He wishes all light was bone white.

He comes out of the curve onto the third floor and he pins the wheels again, goes up the next exit ramp, and he knows that even if the Sequoia has cleared the gate by now, it can't hear his tires in relation to where it would expect them to be. He begins to feel blessed.

He drives up the final exit ramp and reaches the roof. It's near empty up here, and he parks by the first door he sees, trembling and happy. He hopes that someday he has grandchildren and lives to see them just so he can tell them that once he drove up three exit ramps in a parking garage and never hit another car.

He steps out of the car and faces the door.

There's a sign on the door that reads TURN RIGHT, and he almost does, and then he realizes the sign could be referring to the door-knob, so he turns that to the right first, and the door opens.

Just to be sure, he turns his body to the right, sees nothing but

rooftop and then a ledge and then the hospital complex spread beyond the roof in industrial patinas of sandstone and white brick
and eggshell window squares.

So it was the knob.

He walks down two flights of stairs and sees another sign:
CONCOURSE TO GAAR BUILDING. He likes the sound of that—
concourse—so he goes through that door and finds the concourse.
It's more like a breezeway actually, and he crosses it and passes a
doctor and two nurses and a guy in a johnny leading his IV-stand
across the carpet as if it's a slow relative, a pack of cigarettes and a
lighter clenched in his other hand.

A few minutes later, he finds himself in a corridor with bluish
gray carpet. From there, he can see the roof of the parking garage.
The Sequoia sits beside his Honda, hulking. Men in ties stand outside of it. One leans into the Honda and cups his hands on either
side of his face and peers in through the driver's window.

Daniel watches, waiting for something to happen, and he begins
to realize that the men are doing the same thing.

Half an hour later, a black Suburban pulls onto the roof and
parks. Troy gets out of it. He crosses to the other men. There is talking, gesticulating, hands that point vaguely in the direction of the exit
ramp, the door, the sky. In the pointing, Daniel can see their human-
ity, their frustrated ineffectuality, and it comforts him to realize that
these are men who do, in fact, sleep in beds. Have children possibly,
mothers who still harry them, dry-cleaning tickets in their wallets.

Daniel can't be sure from this distance, but Troy seems angry.
At the very least annoyed. He points at Daniel's car in such a way
that Daniel knows it's no longer his. Not in any relevant sense.

They will wait by his car, he is pretty sure. By eluding them, even for a moment, he has broken the unspoken contract. They will watch his house. Tap his phones, if they haven't already. Wait for him in bars.

The wings have stopped flapping in his chest. It feels hollow in there, a basin vulnerable to wind. He resists the urge to sink. To sit on the floor and cover his head with his hands.

He thinks about surrendering or apologizing. He thinks about going down there right now and saying, "I'm sorry. I'm so, so sorry."

But sorry for what? He hasn't done anything. He's just a guy and one day they came looking for him. One day, his name blipped across a screen. One day, he popped up on a list. And that's not his fault. Though he still feels like apologizing. It's natural, he supposes, to not want to be the cause of any sort of ado, any kind of mass consternation. It's a judgment, no matter how nebulous, of your entire life.

But even if he had something to apologize for, he can't. It's too late.

He watches them surrounding his car. They are angry. Pretty soon they will come looking for him. Carrying their anger. He has an image of them walking down the corridor toward him, serving trays held above their shoulders. Waiters. Professional. Indifferent to the cuisine.

HE WANDERS. HE does so, knowing he will be found. He wanders with terror and loneliness caressing the back of his neck and the conviction that he has exiled himself from the world he knew and all her touchstones. He follows signs that intrigue him on some elemental level and ends up outside the SICU. He looks at a few more signs in the corridor. CICU, ICU, NICU. He leans against a wall. Surgical Intensive Care Unit, he decides. An unfortunate acronym, given the location. CICU must be Cardiac Intensive Care Unit, ICU is obvious, but NICU leaves him at a loss. Neurological?

A nurse passes him. She's wearing scrubs with a bright paisley flower print. She looks distracted as she sips from a Subway cup. Daniel can hear the sucking of the straw, down at the bottom, trapped among the ice cubes. She uses the heel of her hand to hit a silver button the size of a cymbal on the wall and the two doors to SICU open, and she tilts her head in his direction and says, "The nurse will find you in the waiting room."

He says, "I'm sorry?"

She jiggles the cup absently. "It's just, you know, we like to keep the corridors clear."

"Sure."

She moves her head slightly, a gesture that Daniel takes to mean that the waiting area is behind him.

"It's okay," she says. "We'll let you know. Soon as we do." Daniel nods and she steps through the doorway and the doors close behind her.

A few minutes later, a young woman, maybe twenty-five, trots past him and stops outside the door. She's dressed for a night out. She smells of perfume and liqueur. She's pudgy, addled, made luminous by fear.

There's a sign over the cymbal-button that says DO NOT ENTER SICU WITHOUT CONTACTING NURSE STATION. LIFT PHONE.

The phone is to the right of the button and the woman lifts it and waits and presses her forehead to the wall and closes her eyes and then jerks back and speaks into the phone, stumbling, cowed:

"Yes. Yes? This is Mr. Brookner's wife. Paul Brookner? I'm his wife. I got a call. I'm . . . I'm Paul Brookner's wife. Oh? Okay."

She hangs up and steps back from the wall, stands in front of the doors and presses the button and tilts her head back for a moment like she's waiting to be beamed up, and the doors open and she tugs her blouse down over her skirt and touches her neck and the underside of her chin with splayed fingers.

She walks through the doors and Daniel feels crushed for her and her tragedy, whatever it may be, a sweeping empathy he rarely feels for the people he knows.

Ten minutes later, a man in a tie comes down the hall toward him. Daniel lowers his head, looks at his shoes. The man comes abreast of him, and Daniel watches his cuffs swing past him and the man turns to his right and enters the ICU.

Daniel breathes, and a small man with a Slavic accent says, "How are you?"

Daniel focuses. The man is too close. He is about fifty years old. He is short and wears a blue barracuda jacket with red lining over a white pinstripe shirt open at the collar and black jeans.

Daniel says, "Excuse me?"

The man peers up at him. "Are you okay?"

"I'm okay." Daniel can hear a defensiveness in the words he didn't intend.

"Who is it?"

"Who is what?"

The man's eyes gesture over Daniel's shoulder. "You're here to see?"

"My father," Daniel says, not sure why.

"He is sick, yes?"

Daniel nods.

"Of?"

Daniel wishes the guy would take a step back. "I really don't want to discuss it."

The man places a soft hand on his wrist. "It's good to talk. Yes? I think it is. My mother. She is here." The man's head tilts in the direction of the ICU.

"What is it?"

"Pneumonia." The man shrugs, as if indifferent to the particulars.

Daniel says, "Open-heart surgery. My father. Things went wrong."

The man nods, and his eyes are tender. He holds out his hand. "My name is Michael."

Daniel shakes the hand. "Daniel."

"My mother?" Michael says. "She is old. Ninety-six. But she is my mother, you see? Ninety-six, a hundred and six, what difference? She is my mother. She is sick." His hands shake slightly. "Your father?"

Daniel takes a moment to compose himself. He's beginning to believe his story, to feel his father is in there, hooked up to tubes, hoses, beeping boxes.

"He's seventy-eight," Daniel says. "He's a strong man."

Michael nods and claps his shoulder. "Now you must be the

strong son. Strong for him. It is this way with things sometimes."
He leans against the wall. "Ah, the waiting." He sighs and drums
his fingers on his thighs.

AT TWO IN the morning, he looks out another window and he
can see them on the roof by his car. Two of them. One takes the
night air. He leans against the grille of the Sequoia and smokes a
cigarette.

Daniel goes back to the ICU waiting room. It's the waiting
room for all the units on the floor. Someone must have figured that
when it came to the loved ones, no S or C or N was necessary. At
this point, it's all ICU.

He is alone except for a Brazilian woman who snores under the
TV, pieces of the Sunday paper scattered at her feet.

He has been here for four hours. Doctors and nurses come and
go but pay attention only to the families of their own patients.
Strange faces, it is assumed, are the problems of other nurses, other
doctors.

Daniel pulls a chair close to the one he's sitting in. He does so
carefully, quietly, so as not to wake the Brazilian woman whose
name he has forgotten. She is here for her husband; he was in a car
accident. Glass wedged in his throat, pieces of plastic from the underside of the dashboard infiltrated his stomach. His surgery has
been going on for five hours. They have no children. He works two
jobs, sends the money home to a brother. He and the brother hope
to open a gas station in two years outside São Paulo. Then, she told
Daniel, they will have children.

Daniel places his feet up on the chair. He places his coat over his chest. He feels the need for sleep as he hasn't since he was a child. He feels that today he has developed a kinship with grief and trauma and nurses' asses. He feels it in his bones: love—for the pudgy woman who'd come from a party, for Michael, for the Brazilian woman, her nose pepper-spangled with dark freckles. He feels flushed with it and exhausted by it. But it's a good exhaustion, earned, he feels.

HE STAYS IN the hospital complex for a month.

At some point, they tow his car. But they don't leave. He sees Troy ten days in, wandering the main street, eyes glancing up at the windows. He rotates to a different hospital every day, returning to the first every seventh. He wanders into ICUs, SICUs, CICUs, even NICUs, which have nothing to do with brain trauma and everything to do with babies, some of them the size of peanuts as they lie under egg-shaped glass, huff into masks, writhe their fists and feet into the air.

It is assumed he is a father, a husband, a brother, and while he has been all those things in his life, he has never felt those roles so proudly or direly as he does here.

He watches the war in waiting rooms with the loved ones of the injured, the impaired, the damaged and broken and internally soupy, the brain-dead, the cancer-stricken, sickle-cell-stricken, terminally anemic, HIV positive, jaundiced, tumor-ridden. He hears stories of rare diseases with odd names. He hears of sudden flicks-of-the-switch in the cerebral cortex, the aorta, the left and right ventricles, the kidneys and pancreas. (And of these, he learns that more than anything, you should pray for a healthy pancreas. Once it goes wrong down there, modern medicine pretty much skips the rest of the show.)

Take care of your colon too. Exercise, for God's sakes. Stay away from the fried food, the cigarettes and liquor, asbestos.

But there's more—don't cross streets where the noon sun is sure to hit the windshields bearing down on you. Don't swim drunk. Don't swim at night. Don't swim. Don't work on the electrical yourself. Don't anally pleasure yourself with a Coke bottle (a rumor, true, going around one of the surgical wards, but a good one; everyone gets a laugh). Don't ski anywhere near trees. Don't live alone. Don't climb a stepladder while pregnant. Don't laugh while eating. And whatever you do, don't retire. Half the people in here are less than a year removed from retirement, and Daniel hears the same tragic-comic stories night after night. He'd taken up fishing, he tended to his garden, he'd been planning a trip, she loved lemonade, she went on long walks, she was knitting an afghan the size of your house, he bought into a time-share, they took up golf.

Daniel watches the war and feels cocooned here. Hospitals strip a lot from you—your independence, your confidence, sometimes your will to live. But pettiness too. Pettiness is the first casualty of the ICU waiting room. No one has the energy for it.

Would you like this magazine? I'm done with it.

Oh, let me remove my coat. Take the seat, take it.

I'm going to get a soda. Would you like one?

Is this okay, or should I keep flipping?

Even the employees in the gift shops and the cafeterias and the food court and at the coffee carts are, to a person, respectful and courteous. Never solicitous, but kind. Because they don't know if your son just died, your wife just received chemo, you've been told you won't see June.

There is a basic human concern in hospitals, a unity. And he begins to suspect he is addicted to it.

HE IS NOT there when Isabella takes Manuelo home after three weeks, but he hears the prognosis is good. But he is there when Michael gets the news that his mother has passed on, and he sits with him on the heating grate of a windowsill overlooking the city. Michael speaks softly of the flower beds she placed in boxes outside her apartment windows, speaks of her need to bake in times of grief, her inclination to purse her lips and go silent in times of joy. He tells Daniel she learned only the most rudimentary English, enough to get her green card, and then never spoke it again except to order meat from the deli.

"She would say, she would say, 'Russia is my home. I did not choose the men who ruined it, who made me leave it. So I do not choose to face that I am not there.'" He claps Daniel's knee. "Ah, she was a rough old woman. Farm stock, you see? Thick ankles, thick head."

Daniel goes down in the elevator with him and they walk outside. It's late, the streets silent and smooth with rain. Michael gives him his card. He is an instructor in martial arts.

"Karate?"

He shakes his head. "Soviet military techniques. No pretty philosophy, just attack."

"You were in the military?"

Michael smiles and lights a cigarette. "I was KGB, my young friend."

Before Daniel can think how to respond, Michael says, "It's so nice to be able to say, yes? I was KGB. Just like that. I say it. It is said." He raises his hands to the air. "And no one stops me. This country . . ."

Daniel says, "I'm not sure you'd get the same result if you said you were CIA."

Michael keeps his smile and nods. He blows smoke into the air and follows it with his chin. "You have no father here."

Daniel says, "I do."

Michael chuckles and shakes his head at his cigarette.

Daniel says, "I don't. Okay."

"You are hiding. Yes?"

Daniel nods.

Michael says, "You will run out of space."

Daniel looks around at the sprawl of buildings. "Eventually."

"But by then—yes?—they could have stopped looking."

A thought infiltrates Daniel before he can stop it: What would I do then?

He says, "They stop looking sometimes, do they?"

Michael nods. "It depends on the level of the offense. But, yes, oftentimes, they just go away."

"To where?"

"Other things. Other files. You wake up one day and there is no one watching anymore."

"Wouldn't that be nice?" Daniel says, but his throat fills with throbs at the prospect.

"And you are free again, yes?"

"Yes."

Michael touches his arm, squeezes it to the bone. "I promised my mother I would take her home."

"To Russia."

He nods, still holding Daniel's arm.

"But this," Michael says, "this is home, I think."

Daniel nods, though he's not sure he understands, and Michael lets go of his arm.

Michael strips the coal off his cigarette with a slide of his finger and thumb, tosses the remains into a trash can. He sniffs the air.

He looks at Daniel. He says, "You have been my friend."

"You've been mine."

Michael shrugs.

"You have."

Another shrug, smaller.

Michael says, "Eventually . . ."

"Yes."

"One way or the other."

"Yes."

Michael smiles that soft smile of his. He takes both of Daniel's shoulders in his hands. He squeezes them and his jaw is clenched below his smile and he looks into Daniel's eyes and nods.

"Good night, my friend."

"Good night."

Daniel stands on the sidewalk. He can smell the rain in the night, though it has long since stopped falling, and he feels the hospital complex breathing around him.

If they really did stop looking . . .

If they really have lost interest altogether . . .

Michael reaches the corner and looks back, gives him a final wave, and Daniel waves back. An ambulance bleats. Lights come on in windows. Out on the main avenue, cars turn right, turn left, beep their horns. Two nurses pass him, one of them laughing as she tries to tell a story. They're on their way somewhere, the local bar for nurses and doctors, he supposes. Or maybe not. Maybe to a restaurant. Maybe home. A movie.

Somewhere.

GONE DOWN TO CORPUS

THAT SUNDAY AFTERNOON, I go up the walk to Lyle Biddet's house and ring the doorbell. I'm hoping Lyle answers and not his mother or father, because I really don't want to think of him as someone's son. I want Lyle to answer the door so I can convince him, real friendly-like, that we're having an off-the-cuff celebration to commemorate our four years playing football together for East Lake High. I'll tell Lyle there are no hard feelings for him dropping that pass on the one and coughing up the ball on the thirty. No hard feelings at all. And Lyle'll follow me back down the walk where Terry Twombley waits behind the wheel of his Cougar with the Lewis brothers sitting in back, and we'll take Lyle on a little ride and find someplace real quiet and kick the shit out of him.

Ain't much of a plan, I know. Best I could come up with after months of stewing on it, though, which again, ain't saying much. Only time I was ever much of a planner was on the football field, and that's over now, over and done, which is pretty much the reason we need to beat up on Lyle, the dumb fuck with the bad hands and all.

Lyle lives in this new suburb called Crescent Shores where there ain't no body of water, ain't no shore, ain't much of anything but all these shiny white houses that all look alike on these shiny white streets that all look alike, which is how come we got lost about six times trying to find his house until one of the Lewis brothers remembered there was a plastic squirrel glued to the roof of the Biddets' mailbox.

I ring the doorbell a second time. It's raining, the drops soft and sweaty, and there don't seem to be anyone around on the whole street. It's like they all left their white houses at the same time and drove off to the same golf tournament. So I turn the knob to the Biddets' front door and—I ain't shitting—it opens. Just like that. I look back over my shoulder at Terry. He sees the open door and his big grin lights up the whole car.

It's been three weeks since graduation. Fourth of July weekend, 1970. I'm eighteen years old.

MY DADDY FOUGHT in Korea. Only thing he ever says about it is that it was cold. Colder'n an icebox. He lost a finger to the cold. Lost half a thumb. In the summer, when everyone is hiding from the sun in dark rooms and under trees and tin porch awnings, my old man's lying out in the backyard with a cooler of beer beside him, eyes closed, chin tilted up. One time, my mother looks out the window at him and gives me a small, broken smile. "Damn," she says, "but he looked fine in a uniform."

———

TERRY AND THE Lewis brothers park the Cougar a block over and then come back to the house, streak up the walk and inside, and I shut the door behind them. It's cool in the house, the air blowing from these vents cut high up in the walls, and for a minute we all walk around looking at the vents, marveling. Morton Lewis says, "I gotta get me a setup like this."

His brother Vaughn goes, "Shit. We take just *one* of those vents, it'll be good enough for our whole place."

He actually climbs up on the couch, looks like he's fixing to rip one out of the wall, take it home with him. I can picture him a few hours later with the thing sitting in front of him on the kitchen table, trying to find a place for the batteries.

You put the brains of both Lewis brothers together and you still come up with something dumber than a barrel of roofing tar, but those boys are also tear-ass fast and my-daddy's-a-mean-drunk crazy off the snap count, kinda boys can turn a starting left tackle into the town gimp, come back to the huddle not even breathing hard.

Terry says, "Nice house," and walks around the living room looking at everything. "Got a bar too."

There's a small swimming pool out back. It's the shape of a jellyfish and, like I said, none too big, but we have a few drinks from the bar and then we all go out and piss in it.

That's what gets us going, I think. We go back into that too-white house and the Lewis brothers have at the vents, and I push over a vase in the dining room, and Terry breaks all the knobs off the TV and pours his beer all over the couch and we go on smashing and tearing things for a while, drunk from the liquor, but drunk with something else too, a kind of hysteria, I think, a need to keep from crying.

IF WE'D WON that last game of the season, we would have gone on to the divisional playoffs against Lubbock Vo-Tech. Only way college scouts see you if you grow up in a tiny shithole like ours is if you make it to the divisionals. And that's where we were heading, no question, until Lyle Biddet's hands turned to Styrofoam. He coughed up the ball twice—once on the fucking *one*—and North Park converted both of Biddet's gifts into touchdowns, left us standing numb and cold under a black Texas sky, fans heading home, the lights shutting off.

My guidance counselor asks me a week later what I plan to make out of my life, what I'm fixing to do with it, what I plan to apply myself to, and all I'm thinking is: I want to *apply* my hands to Lyle Biddet's throat, keep squeezing till they cramp up.

Lyle, you see, never needed the divisional game. He was going to college no matter what. SMU, I hear. Nice school.

WE'VE OBLITERATED MOST of the first floor by the time the girl walks in. The hi-fi is in the swimming pool along with two shredded leather armchairs. The fridge is doors-open and tits-down on the kitchen floor. Potted plants are unpotted, the toilet's spilling into the hall, and don't even ask what the Lewis brothers added to the chocolate rug pattern.

So we're standing there, kind of spent all of a sudden, amazed as we look around a bit and see how much shit we managed to fuck up in forty minutes and with no one ever giving the order. That was the weirdest thing—how it just *happened.* It just sprung up, like it had a mind of its own, and that mind went apeshit and angry all over the Biddets' house.

And then the side door off the kitchen opens and she walks in. Her dirty blond hair is combed straight down but with two matching strands braided and hanging over her small ears. She's got white boots going up to her knees, and above that she's wearing one of those plaid schoolgirl skirts they wear in the private, Jesus schools, except hers has got red finger-paint splattered on it and someone's drawn a peace symbol over the left thigh. Her T-shirt is tight and I can just make out a pair of hard little nipples pressing up against the tie-dye.

I've seen her a couple times before, when she was younger— Lyle's little sister, a year behind us. She'd gone to East Lake her first year, but then we heard rumors of trouble, a boyfriend in his twenties, a suicide attempt, some said, and the next year she didn't come back, got shipped to someplace outside of Dallas, supposedly, locked up with the nuns.

She stops by the overturned fridge, looking down at it for a second like she isn't sure it belongs there, and then she looks up and sees us. She doesn't scream. For a second, I see something catch in her face. A word enters her eyes, and I know exactly what the word is: rape.

I see her throat move as she swallows, and then she says, "You all done fucking up my momma's house? Or you just getting started?"

She's looking at me when she says it, and I can hear Terry and the Lewis brothers breathing real shallow-like behind me.

She ain't mad or nothing. I can see that. She ain't appalled that we destroyed her house. In fact, as she holds her eyes on mine, I can see she's maybe thought about doing this herself once or twice, maybe came back here for that very reason.

I say, "You're Lurlene, right?"

She steps up on the back of the fridge, arms out for balance, just one toe up there, her other leg out in the air. She nods, looking down at the heating coils. "And you're Mister Quarterback man, ain't you? East Lake BMOC, all that shit?" She's looking at the fridge below her, a small smile creeping up her thin face, and she draws *shit* out in that Texas woman's way, makes it sound as wide as a field.

"Ma'am." I lift an imaginary Stetson off my head.

The way she's doing that balancing act atop the overturned fridge just kills me for some reason. There's four strange boys standing in her house, and the house looks like them boys rolled a grenade through it, but she's up there doing her ballerina act and somehow taking control of the situation by acting like there ain't really much of a situation to speak of. She just sucks the breath from my chest, I'll tell you what.

She looks out past my shoulder at the living room and whispers, "Dang. You all fucked this place up."

Terry stutters. He says, "We didn't mean to, miss."

She hops off the fridge, lands beside me, but keeps her eyes on Terry. "Didn't mean to? Boy, I'd hate to see what you could do, you had a *mind* to."

Terry laughs and drops his eyes.

"Any liquor left?" She moves into the living room and I follow. "Sure."

"I'd like me a tequila," she says, moving toward the bar, about the only thing left standing. "And then we can all go to work on the upstairs. What you say?"

SOMETIMES, AFTER THE sun's gone down and Daddy's been sitting out back all day drinking Lone Stars and adding some sour mash to the mix too, he'll end up looking at his shitty house and sloping back porch and hard Texas dirt and he'll cry without a sound. He'll sit there, not moving or shaking or nothing, just sit rock-still, his face leaking.

Says to me once, he says, "I'd known this was what it was all about, boy, know what I'd a done?"

I'm maybe ten. I say, "No, Daddy."

He takes a long pull on a can, tosses it aside, and belches. "Died earlier."

WE'RE UP IN Mr. and Mrs. Biddet's bedroom, taking a butcher knife to the big, fluffy, four-poster bed, just me and Lurlene. Terry and the Lewis brothers are in Lyle's room and by the sounds of it, they're tearing that place down to the fucking studs. For some reason, I'm not as mad at Lyle as I was when we came here, hell, as I was the whole winter and spring. I'm still mad, though. Madder than ever maybe. But it's something besides Lyle I'm mad at, something I can't put a name to. Something out there that hulks over the flat land like a dinosaur shadow, something bigger than Lyle and bigger than Texas, maybe. Something huge.

Lurlene's done tore hell out of all four pillows, and it hits me as the room fills with feathers, a blizzard of them swirling between me and Lurlene, sticking to her hair and eyelashes, me spitting them off my tongue—it hits me and I say it:

"How do we know when they're coming back?"

Lurlene laughs at me and blows at some swirling feathers and arches her back to catch some of the blizzard on her throat.

"They're gone down to Corpus, boy. Hell," she says, drawing it out the same way she drew out *shit*, teasing the word, "they won't be back till late Monday. They go every weekend come summer. Them and their precious Lyle."

"Gone down to Corpus," I say.

"Gone down to Corpus!" She shrieks and hits me with what's left of a pillow, the down spilling into my shirt.

Then she drops to all fours and crawls across the bed to me and says, "You think this is a rich house, boy?"

I nod, my throat drying up, her green eyes so soft and close.

"This ain't nothing," she says. "How'd you like to go to a house four times this size? Do four times the damage?"

Seems like I forget how to speak for a minute. Lurlene and her green eyes and too-thin face and body have slid into me somehow, under the flesh, under the bone. I'm about certain I've never seen any creature so beautiful as this girl with the butcher knife in her hand and that crazed laugh in her pupils. You can see hope living in her—anxious, lunatic hope, but pure and kind too, wanting only to be met halfway.

She says, "Huh, boy? You want to?"

I nod again. Ain't doing much with myself anyway, and suddenly, I'm pretty sure I'll follow Lurlene anywhere she says. Bust up anything she wants. The whole goddamn world if she asks me nice.

ABOUT FIVE YEARS back, we break down on Route 39, just me and my mother, and we're standing there in the white heat with the dirt, dying of thirst for a hundred flat miles in every direction and Daddy's piece-of-shit truck gone gasping into a coma beside us, and my mother puts a hand over her eyebrows to scan the emptiness and she looks like any fight left in her just up and died with the truck. She looks like she can remember a time before she got where she is now, and all those different who-she-could-have-beens fork out like trails before us, branching off and branching off into all that Texas dust until there's so many of them they just have to fade away to nothing or else she'll go blind trying to keep count.

Her voice is dry and torn when she speaks, and it takes a couple breaths to get the words out:

"Remember, Sonny, times like these—remember that somewhere there's someone worse off than you. You're always richer than someone." She tries for a smile as she looks over at me. "Right?"

POORER, I'M THINKING as we get back in the Cougar and follow Lurlene's directions to this other house. You're always poorer than someone. And that poor is a high fence keeping you out of all the places other people can go. Only places you get to go are the shitty ones nobody else wants to visit.

Always poorer, I'm thinking, and then we reach this house Lurlene's directing us to, and I'm suddenly thinking, Maybe not.

Because whoever owns this house may not be poorer than anyone. Whoever owns this house may be the richest person in the world.

The front lawn is bigger than East Lake's football field. The house behind it is sprawling and beige with a red tile roof and it seems to spread itself from end to end like a god.

We come up to a tall, wrought-iron gate stretched between two beige brick columns that match the house. The gate is a good twenty feet high, and even with all the tequila-and-beer courage I got from the Biddets', I can tell you I feel nothing but relief when I see that gate and realize we ain't getting in. I see it in Terry's face too, even though he says, "So now what do we do?"

Lurlene's sitting on the console between us, hunched forward, skinny arms wrapped around her knees. She takes a last swig from a bottle of Cuervo and hands it to Terry. I'm ready for her to say, "Drive through it." I'm ready for her to say anything. I might not like it. But I'm ready.

All she says, though, is, "Could I get by, kind sir?" and slithers over my lap and out the door.

She saunters up to the gate in her white boots and tarnished schoolgirl skirt and behind me, Vaughn Lewis says, "I'm fucked up."

"Me too," his brother says.

I look at Terry. He shrugs, but I can see the booze swimming in him, making his eyelids thicken and squiggle.

Lurlene finds this box sticking out of the column on our left. There's numbers on it, and her fingers dance over them and then she's heading back to the car as the gate begins to open, just starts sliding back into the bushes behind the column on our right. Lurlene hops in and sits in my lap, tosses an arm around my neck and looks out through the windshield as the gate goes all the way back.

She tells Terry, "Time to put it in 'drive.'"

THERE'S A PICTURE of my parents taken just before they got married. It's 1949 and my daddy's wearing his uniform. It's all neat and sharply creased, and his hair is short and slicked back, and he has all his teeth. He's beaming this white, white smile, holding my mother so tight with one arm that she looks about to bust in half. She's smiling too, though, and it's a real smile. She was happy then. Happier than I've ever seen her. She's young. They're both young. They look younger than me. Behind them is a chain-link fence with a sign on it that says FORT BENNING, GA. My mother's dress is white with a pattern of what looks like black swallows on it, those swallows soaring across her body.

And, man, she's happy. She's happy, and my daddy has all his teeth and all his fingers.

LURLENE GETS US in the house the same way she got us through the gate. Her fingers dart across these numbers on a gizmo beside the front door and then we're inside.

We walk around for a while. Ain't none of us, except Lurlene maybe, ever seen a house this big. Ain't sure any of us knew there was a house this big. The front hall has two staircases that meet at a curve up top. It's got a chandelier the size of a fucking Cadillac and all these vases that're taller than any of us, including Terry, and the walls leading up the staircases are lined with paintings in gold, frilly frames.

On the second floor, there's a ballroom, Lord's sake. And past that, a room with a long bar and a pool table twice as big as the one in the Biddets' house with these leather sacks for pockets. In the guy's study there's a desk you could sleep on and never worry about rolling off. There's another bar in there and bookcases lining the walls and the ceilings go up a good fifteen feet and there are ladders on rollers for the cases. I go up to that desk and there's a picture of this guy with his wife and two kids and another of him on a golf course and another of him, Jesus Christ, shaking hands with Lyndon Baines, himself. The King of Texas. Man who walked away from the Big Job and said, Fuck it. I ain't no president. I'm a Longhorn. You all fight the war on poverty and the war against the yellow folk, I'm going home.

I say to Lurlene, "Who *are* these folks?"

Lurlene sits up on the corner of the desk. She picks up the picture with the guy and LBJ. She holds it by the corner in one hand, her wrist bending back, and for a second, I think she's going to throw it across the room.

She puts it back, though. Right where she picked it up from. Exactly. Maybe it's all the dark oak in there or the red-wine leather chairs, or all those thick book spines staring down at us. Else, maybe it's just LBJ staring out from that photograph, at us, but I know all of a sudden that we ain't going to touch this room. Ain't going to do a damn thing to it. The rest of the house, maybe, but not this room.

Lurlene says, "I go to school with the daughter."

I look at the pudgy guy with LBJ. "*His* daughter?"

"She was my friend at Saint Mary's." She fingers the hem of her skirt. She looks up at the high ceilings and shrugs. "She ain't my friend no more, though. She ain't nothing but shit."

She hops off the desk and I can see that her eyes are wet, not much, but wet just the same, and a little red. She places her palm on my chest as she passes and gives me a peck on the cheek.

"Come on," she says. "Let's go downstairs. See how much destruction your friends done."

MY GRADUATION, MY mother gives me twenty dollars she's managed to tuck away. She tells me to go have some fun, I been getting too serious.

Daddy gives me his old truck. Same one broke down on my mother and me that time. Says to me: She's all mine.

I spend a week patching that old bitch together, blow the whole twenty dollars in junkyards on hoses and bushings, a distributor cap.

The afternoon I get it running, I take a few of my father's Lone Stars and chase a red sky across miles of scrub gone purple with the dusk. I pull over in the middle of all this nothing, and I sit on the hood, and I drink down those beers one after the other until the world's gone dark around me. And I wonder what the fuck's going to become of me. I wonder what I'm supposed to do now. Got me a useless truck and a useless high school diploma. I should be like my parents were in that 1949 picture, all smiling and hopeful and shit. But I ain't. What's waiting for me out there, out past the dark and the whole of Texas, ain't nothing I'm looking forward to. And what's waiting behind me don't amount to anything neither but what stole those smiles off my parents' faces.

I lean back on the hood. I look up at the stars. I look up at the black, black sky. It's so quiet. And I think about what my daddy said about how he would have died earlier had he known what the world was going to bring. And I sort of get that now. I sort of do.

To die. But not by my own hand. And not by some yellow man's neither. But somehow. In a big blaze that'll light up the dark sky. Something like that.

COMING DOWN THE stairs, me and Lurlene are wondering just what the other boys have been getting up to, imagining a big rich house turned into a squatter's shack in the fifteen minutes we've been gone, but when we turn into the living room past that gigantic entry hall, we find Terry and the Lewis brothers just standing around, fidgeting, and I can tell by the cushions on the three different couches in there that they ain't even tried to sit down. They just been standing there the whole time, hands in their pockets or wiping against their jeans, and the moment I walk in, Terry says, "We don't like it here."

I say, "How come?"

He shrugs, his eyes wide. He's kind of crouching a bit, shoulders tensed like he expects the ceiling to come crashing down on him. "Don't know. Just don't. Ain't no place to set."

I look around at all the couches and antique chairs. "Ain't no place to—?"

"We just don't like it," Vaughn Lewis says. "We just don't like it at all."

Vaughn too is all tensed up, his eyes darting around, like he expects something with teeth and claws to charge him.

"We're fixing to go," Terry tells me.

"I want to look around some more," I say, though I'm not sure I do.

"Come on," Lurlene says. "We got some damage to do!"

Terry shakes his head. "Ain't wanna touch nothing in this here house."

I look at Vaughn and Morton. They both look ready to dive out the window.

And I can feel it too. Ain't nothing here but an empty house, but it's some mean house. Some big, mean, icy house. Too clean, too gleaming, ready to swallow us all.

Terry says, "We gone git, son." He steps up to me, meets my eyes. "Got to git. Got to."

I say, "Okay. Git then."

"You coming?"

I look at Lurlene. The hope in those green eyes has gotten bigger and more desperate.

I say, "No. You boys git along. I'll catch up."

"You sure?"

I meet his eyes and nod. "We'll see you."

They each give Lurlene a shy nod as they leave, but they can't get out of there quick enough. Seems half a second after they close the door behind them, I hear the Cougar roar out of there.

"The gate," I say.

Lurlene shakes her head. "You on the inside, it opens by itself as you approach it. You on the outside . . ." She shrugs and walks around the living room looking at stuff.

I wander into a den and open up a gun cabinet. I look at all these beautiful shotguns with carvings on the barrels and in the stocks, but I don't touch them. I go to the next cabinet and look at the handguns. I find one I like. It's a black Walther with a bone white handle. Fits in my hand real nice. I drop the magazine into my palm, even though I can tell from the weight that it's loaded. I slide the magazine back in. It's the first thing in the house I've touched, and for a second I see my mother with her hand over her eyes as she looks off across miles of scrub and dead land, and I put that Walther behind my back and walk out of the room.

Me and Lurlene wander the house for the next hour and I don't think we see but half of it. She shows me the scars on her wrists at one point, tells me it wasn't but a "cry out." Still, she says, all that blood on the bathroom tile. Like you never saw, she says. Like you'd never want to.

We find a bedroom that's got its own TV and a walk-in closet and dolls piled to the ceiling atop this wide dresser. There's a hi-fi in there and pictures on the walls of Davy Jones and Bobby Sherman and Paul McCartney, and I know we're in the girl's room, the one who used to be Lurlene's friend.

We stand in the doorway and I say, "You want to bust it up?"

And Lurlene says, "I want to."

I start to walk in. "Then let's—"

She pulls me back. She sags into me. She says, "No," in a sad crush of a voice.

I hold her as we wander around some more and eventually work our way back downstairs to the kitchen. There's a staircase off the kitchen, kind of tucked away by the pantry, and we follow it down. We find a bedroom down there with a tiny bathroom and its own small kitchen. About the only small things I've seen in this whole house. The walls in the bedroom are bare, but there's women's clothes in the closet. Not the kind of clothes you expect to see in a house like this, kind of threadbare, Woolworth labels and the like.

The bed is small too, and we lie down on top of the covers, and for some reason, I feel comfortable for the first time since I entered this monster. I lie there with Lurlene and after a while she says, "How come we couldn't do nothing?"

"I don't know."

"How come we didn't even *try*?"

I say it again: "I don't know."

"She talked trash about me at school," she says. "Told people I was cheap. Made fun of my clothes. Said I was common." She slides an arm across my chest and holds on tight. "I'm not common. I'm not shit."

I kiss her forehead and hold her.

"You still gone beat up Lyle?"

"No," I say.

"Why?" She gives me those green eyes and they seem bigger as they look down into mine.

I get a picture of the jungle for some reason, a world of green leaves, dripping. I see John Wayne telling that little yellow kid in *The Green Berets*, "You're what this is all about," and I think how I don't have no fight left in me. I think how John Wayne is full of shit.

I pull the gun out from behind my back and place it on the bed beside me, wonder what'll happen if we hear the sudden turn of a key in the front door lock upstairs, the rich family coming home and us down here hiding in the bed like a pair of big bad wolves waiting for Goldilocks. I wonder what I'll do then. Make that pudgy man in the picture go get one of his shotguns maybe. Make that pudgy man draw. I don't know. I know that at the moment I hate the pudgy man more than I hate Lyle.

And, yet, it was Lyle's house I fucked up. And I know I ain't going to do nothing to the pudgy man's house except wait down here with his gun. Why that is, I can't rightly tell you. But I feel ashamed.

I see my daddy out in the backyard, his face leaking, and I see my mother with that hand over her eyes, and I see the red sky I chased in that shitty truck. I see John Wayne in the jungle and LBJ in that picture and Lurlene standing up on the fridge, ballerina-like, and I see Lyle dropping that ball on the one, and those stands gone empty of fans under the black sky, and I think how it would have been nice for someone besides my dumb, drunk daddy to have told me that this is it. This is the whole deal.

"Maybe we should go down to Corpus," I say.

Lurlene curls into me. "That'd be nice."

"Just go down," I say. "Disappear."

Lurlene's hand runs over my chest. "Disappear," she says.

But we don't move. We lie there, the house quiet all around us, the quiet of a sleeping baby's lung. We listen for a sound, a click, a generator's hum. But there's nothing, not even a bed creak as Lurlene shifts her body a little more and places her ear to my chest and pulls my hand between her breasts. I can't feel her heartbeat, though. Can't feel my own, either, my chest gone still as the house as she lies against me, listening for the sound of my heart. Waiting and listening. Listening and waiting. For the steady beat, I guess. The dull roar.

MUSHROOMS

HER BOYFRIEND, KL, is driving, and she and Sylvester are packed beside him in the front seat of the Escalade, sucking down Lites as they drive through the rain from Dorchester, Massachusetts, to Hampton Beach, New Hampshire. Every twenty miles or so, KL reaches over her shoulder and taps Sylvester's neck and says, "Sylvester, you know my girlfriend, right?" until Sylvester finally says, "Hey, KL. Okay. We've met."

She and KL dropped two hits of GHB just before they picked Sylvester up, and she thinks it's starting to show. She keeps touching her face with sweaty hands and giggling because they've forgotten the bullets and it's been a long time since she's seen the ocean and here it is raining and because KL keeps flinching every time a puddle explodes against his silver rims.

"KL," Sylvester says, "this girl is fucked up."

She says, "Sylvester, your nose is weird. Anyone ever tell you that? One nostril is tiny. And the other is, like, jet-engine size." She tries to touch his nose.

"Serious, KL," Sylvester says. "Fucked up."

KL says to him, "Relax. Find something on the radio, look at the scenery, do some fucking thing."

Sylvester rests the side of his forehead against the window and stares out at the rain snapping off the highway, boiling in puddles.

When they reach the beach, it's empty, even the boardwalk, just like KL figured. They sit on the seawall and KL gives her his pissed-off glare. She can't tell if he's pissed off because she left the bullets in her other jacket or if he's still part-pissed about the whole situation in general. Eventually, he gives her a smile when she raises her right eyebrow. He kisses her and his tongue tastes like metal because of the GHB and then he says, "Sylvester, come smoke this with me." He and Sylvester walk down the beach in the rain and she sits on the wall in the cold and watches while they walk into the ocean and KL holds Sylvester under the water until he drowns.

HE HANDS HER the gun when he gets back, tells her to hold on to it.

She says, "That's kind of risky, don't you think?"

He puts his thumbs under her eyelids and pulls them down, looks into her eyes. "Drugs making you paranoid. That's a good gun."

They walk the beach for a bit as KL tells her how he did it, how he bluffed with the gun, put it against Sylvester's head and forced him down into the water. "I tell him I'm just going to teach him a lesson, hold him down for a minute because he fucked up with Whitehall and that Rory thing too."

"He believe you?"

KL smiles, kind of surprised himself. "For a few seconds, yeah. After that, it didn't much matter."

She watches the water to see if Sylvester pops up anywhere, but the waves are cold and gray and high, like whales, and KL tells her there was a pretty strong undertow out there too. Clams, a few inches below the wet sand, spit on her feet as she stares at the sea and KL wraps his arms around her from behind. She leans back into his chest, the heat of it, and KL says, "I had a dream about killing him last night. How it would feel."

"And?"

He shrugs. "Wasn't much different."

SHE WASN'T ALWAYS old.

Not long ago she was a girl, a girl without breasts, with a little boy's body really. She walked back from school one day in a skirt she hated—an itchy, woolen thing with pleats, black-and-gray plaid, a chafing thing. She walked alone—usually she was alone— and the streets she followed home were tired, like they'd had a flu too long, the buildings leaning forward as if they'd topple onto her braided hair, her nose, her little boy's body.

She cut through a playground, and there was a man sitting on the jungle gym, drinking a tall can of beer. He wore an army uniform that had sharp creases in the pants even though the shirt was wrinkled. He stood and blocked her path. She met his eyes and saw that there was a kindness hiding in them behind the rest of what lived there, which was good, because the rest of what lived there was hopeless, as if all the light had been vacuumed out. She never knew how long they stared at each other—a day maybe, an hour, a year—but everything changed. Her little boy's body disappeared forever, sucked into those blasted eyes, replaced with a new body, a body that ached, that tingled as he watched her, a body covered with skin so new and thin it felt raw.

He said, "Fuck you waiting for, little girl? A hall pass?" And he bowed and held out his arm and she saw light fill his eyes for an instant, a moment in which she saw how beautiful they could be, powder blue and soft, love living there like a morning prayer. When he caressed her ass as she passed, she resisted the urge to lean into his hand.

When she got home, she saw his eyes in the mirror. She ran a hand over her new body, over the sudden nubs of her breasts, and she knew for the first time why her father sometimes seemed afraid and ashamed when he looked at her. She knew, looking in the mirror, that she was not of him; she was of her mother; she felt buried with her in the dark earth.

The next day, when she walked through the playground, he was waiting. He was smiling, and his shirt had been ironed.

WHAT HAPPENED TO Sylvester was all Rory's fault, really, part of the stupid shit that went on in their neighborhood so much that to keep up with the whos and the whys you'd need a damn score-card.

Rory stole some guy's Zoom LeBrons one night while everyone was goofing in the hydrant spray. When the guy asked around, one of Rory's girlfriends, Lorraine, told the guy it was Rory. Lorraine hated Rory because he'd saddled her with a baby who shit and cried all night and kept her from her friends. So the guy kicked Rory's ass and took his LeBrons back, and one night Rory and his buddy Pearl took Lorraine up to Pope's Hill and caved in her head with a tree branch. Once she was dead, they did some other things too so the police would think it was some psycho and not a neighborhood thing.

Rory told some friends, though; said it was like fucking a fish on ice. And Sylvester heard about it. Sylvester was Lorraine's half brother on the father's side, and one night he and a carload of boys came cruising for Rory.

It was summer and she was sitting on her stoop waiting for KL. Her father was inside snoozing, and her sister, Sonya, was sitting on the big blue mailbox at the head of the alley, saying she was going to tell their father she was seeing KL again, catch her another beat-ing. Sonya was singing it: "I'm a tell Dad-ee / You and KL getting bump-ee."

Then Rory came out of his house and she saw the car come up the street with the windows rolling down and the muzzles sticking out and she began to step off the stoop when the noise started and Sonya floated for a second, as if the breeze had puckered up and kissed her. She floated up off the mailbox and then she flipped side-ways and hit a trash can a few feet back in the alley.

Rory danced against the wall of the Korean deli, parts of him popping, his arms flapping like a stork's.

When she reached Sonya, her sister was covering her kneecaps with her palms. She brushed her hair back out of her eyes and held her shoulders until her teeth stopped chattering, until the tiny whistle-noise coming from her chest stopped all at once, just whistled back into itself and went to sleep.

KL CALLS THEM mushrooms. It's like that old Centipedes game, KL says, where you have to shoot the centipede but those mushrooms keep falling, getting in the way.

Sometimes, KL says, you're aiming for the centipede, but you hit the mushroom.

KL FOUND OUT the Whitehall crew from Franklin Park was looking for Sylvester because he owed them big and hadn't been making payments. When KL told them he knew firsthand that Sylvester had been borrowing elsewhere, Whitehall agreed to his offer. Just do it out of state, they told him. Too many people hoping to tie us to shit.

So KL waited until October and they ended up driving to Hampton Beach with Sylvester, kept going even after she realized she'd forgotten the bullets. Sylvester, leaning his head against the window, so stupid he doesn't even know KL's girlfriend is the sister of the girl on the mailbox. So stupid he thinks

KL's suddenly his best friend, taking him out for a Sunday drive. So stupid.

Period.

ON THE BEACH, she asks KL if he looked into Sylvester's eyes before he made him kneel in the ocean, if maybe he saw anything there.

"Come on," KL says, "just, fuck, shut up, you know?"

SHE'S BEEN OUT to the ocean once before. Not long after KL got back from Afghanistan and she met up with him, he scored off this cop who'd been part of the Lafayette Raiders bust. This cop had known someone who'd served over there with KL, someone who hadn't made it back, and he sold the shit to KL for 40 percent of the street value, called it his "yellow ribbon" price, supporting the troops and shit. KL turned that package over in one night, and the next day they took the ferry to Provincetown.

They walked the dunes and they felt like silk underfoot, large spilling drifts of white silk. They ate lobster and watched the sky darken and become striped with pale pink ribbons. On the ferry back, she could smell the sun in KL's fingers as they played with her hair. She could smell the dunes and the silk sand and the butter that had dripped off the lobster meat. And as the city appeared, all silver glitter and white and yellow light, she could feel the hum and hulk of it wash the smells away. She pressed her palm against KL's hard stomach, felt the cables of muscle under the flesh, and she wished she could still smell it all baked into his skin.

SHE WALKS UP the wet beach with him now and they cross the boardwalk and she thinks of Sonya floating off that mailbox and floating, right now, somewhere beyond this world, looking down, and she feels that her baby sister has grown older too, older than herself, that she has run far ahead of time and its laws. She is wrinkled now and wiser and she does not approve of what they have done.

What they have done needed to be done. She feels sure of that. Someone had to pay, a message had to be sent. Can't have some fool traveling free through life like he got an all-day bus pass. You got to pay the freight. Everyone. Got to.

But still she can feel her sister, looking down on her with a grim set to her mouth, thinking: Stupid. Stupid.

She and KL reach the Escalade and he opens the hatch and she places the gun in there under the mat and the tire iron and the donut spare.

"Never want to hear his name aloud," KL says. "Never again. We clear?"

She nods and they stand there in the sweeping rain.

"What now?" she says.

"Huh?"

"What now?" she repeats, because suddenly she has to know. She has to.

"We go home."

"And then?"

He shrugs. "No then."

"There's gotta be then. There's gotta be something next."

Another shrug. "There ain't."

In the Escalade, KL driving, the rain still coming down, she thinks about going back to school, finishing. She imagines herself in a nurse's uniform, living someplace beyond the neighborhood. She worries she's getting ahead of herself. Don't look so far into the future. Look into the next minute. See it. See that next minute pressing against your face. What can you do with it? With that time? What?

She closes her eyes. She tries to see it. She tries to make it her own. She tries and tries.

UNTIL GWEN

YOUR FATHER PICKS you up from prison in a stolen Dodge Neon with an eight ball in the glove compartment and a hooker named Mandy in the backseat. Two minutes into the ride, the prison still hanging tilted in the rearview, Mandy tells you that she only hooks part-time. The rest of the time she does light secretarial for an independent video chain and tends bar two Sundays a month at the local VFW. But she feels her calling—her true calling in life—is to write.

You go, "Books?"

"Books." She snorts, half out of amusement, half to shoot a line off your fist and up her left nostril. "Screenplays!" She shouts it at the dome light for some reason. "You know—movies."

"Tell him the one about the psycho saint guy," your father says. "That would put my ass in the seat." Your father winks at you in the rearview, like he's driving the two of you to the prom. "Go ahead. Tell him."

"Okay, okay." She turns on the seat to face you, and your knees touch, and you think of Gwen, a look she gave you once, nothing special, just looking back at you as she stood at the front door, asking if you'd seen her keys. A forgettable moment if ever there was one but you spent four years in prison remembering it.

". . . so at his canonization," Mandy is saying, "something, like, happens? And his spirit comes *back* and goes into the body of this priest. But, like, the priest? He has a brain tumor. He doesn't know it or nothing, but he does, and it's fucking up his, um—"

"Brain?" you try.

"Thoughts," Mandy says. "So he gets this saint in him and that *does it*, because like even though the guy was a saint, his spirit has become evil because his soul is gone. So this priest? He spends the rest of the movie trying to kill the pope."

"Why?"

"Just listen," your father says. "It gets good."

You look out the window. A car sits empty along the shoulder. It's beige and someone has painted gold wings on the sides, fanning out from the front bumper and across the doors, and a sign is affixed to the roof with some words on it, but you've passed it by the time you think to wonder what it says.

"See, there's this secret group that works for the Vatican? They're like a, like a . . ."

"A hit squad," your father says.

"Exactly," Mandy says and presses her finger to your nose. "And the lead guy, the, like, head agent? He's the hero. He lost his

wife and daughter in a terrorist attack on the Vatican a few years
back, so he's a little fucked up, but—"

You say, "Terrorists attacked the Vatican?"

"Huh?"

You look at her, waiting. She has a small face, eyes too close to
her nose.

"In the *movie*," Mandy says. "Not in real life."

"Oh. I just, you know, four years inside, you assume you miss a
couple of headlines, but . . ."

"Right." Her face dark and squally now. "Can I finish?"

"I'm just saying," you say and snort another line off your fist,
"even the guys on death row would have heard about that one."

"Just go with it," your father says. "It's not like real life."

You look out the window, see a guy in a chicken suit carrying
a can of gas in the breakdown lane, think how real life isn't like
real life. Probably more like this poor dumb bastard running out
of gas in a car with wings painted on it. Wondering how the hell
he ever got here. Wondering who he'd pissed off in that previous
real life.

YOUR FATHER HAS rented two rooms at an Econo Lodge so
you and Mandy can have some privacy, but you send Mandy home
after she twice interrupts the blow job she's giving you to pontificate on the merits of Michael Bay films.

You sit in the blue-wash flicker of ESPN and eat peanuts from a
plastic sleeve you got out of a vending machine and drink plastic

cupfuls of Jim Beam from a bottle your father presented when you reached the parking lot. You think of the time you've lost and how nice it is to sit alone on a double bed and watch TV, and you think of Gwen, can taste her tongue for just a moment, and you think about the road that's led you here to this motel room on this night after forty-seven months in prison and how a lot of people would say it was a twisted road, a weird one, filled with curves, but you just think of it as a road like any other. You drive down it on faith or because you have no other choice and you find out what it's like by the driving of it, find out what the end looks like only by reaching it.

LATE THE NEXT morning, your father wakes you, tells you he drove Mandy home and you've got things to do, people to see.

Here's what you know about your father above all else—people have a way of vanishing in his company.

He's a professional thief, consummate con man, expert in his field, and yet there's something far beyond professionalism at his core, something unreasonably arbitrary. Something he keeps within himself like a story he heard once, laughed at maybe, yet swore never to repeat.

"She was with you last night?" you say.

"You didn't want her. Somebody had to prop her ego back up. Poor girl like that."

"But you drove her home," you say.

"I'm speaking Czech?"

You hold his eyes for a bit. They're big and bland, with the

heartless innocence of a newborn's. Nothing moves in them, nothing breathes, and after a while you say, "Let me take a shower."

"Fuck the shower," he says. "Throw on a baseball cap and let's
get."

You take the shower anyway, just to feel it, another of those
things you would have realized you'd miss if you'd given it any
thought ahead of time, standing under the spray, no one near you,
all the hot water you want for as long as you want it, shampoo that
doesn't smell like factory smoke.

Drying your hair and brushing your teeth, you can hear the old
man flicking through channels, never pausing on one for more than
thirty seconds: Home Shopping Network—zap. Springer—zap.
Oprah—zap. Soap opera voices; soap opera music—zap. Monster
truck show—pause. Commercial—zap, zap, zap.

You come back into the room, steam trailing you, and pick your
jeans up off the bed, put them on.

The old man says, "Afraid you'd drowned. Worried I'd have to
take a plunger to the drain, suck you back up."

You say, "Where we going?"

"Take a drive," your father says with a small shrug, flicks past a
cartoon.

"Last time you said that, I got shot twice."

Your father looks back over his shoulder at you, eyes big and
soft like a six-year-old's. "Wasn't the car that shot you, was it?"

YOU GO OUT to Gwen's place, but she isn't there anymore, a
couple of black kids playing in the front yard, black mother coming

out on the porch to look at the strange car idling in front of her house.

"You didn't leave it here?" your father says.

"Not that I recall."

"Think."

"I'm thinking."

"So you didn't?"

"I told you—not that I recall."

"So you're sure."

"Pretty much."

"You had a bullet in your head."

"Two."

"I thought one glanced off."

You say, "Two bullets hit your fucking head, old man, you don't get hung up on the particulars."

"That how it works?" Your father pulls away from the curb as the woman comes down the steps.

THE FIRST SHOT came through the back window, and Gentleman Pete flinched big-time, jammed the wheel to the right and drove the car straight into the highway exit barrier, air bags exploding, water barrels exploding, something in the back of your head exploding, glass pebbles filling your shirt, Gwen going, "What happened? Jesus. What happened?"

You pulled her with you out the back door—Gwen, your Gwen—and you crossed the exit ramp and ran into the woods and the second shot hit you there but you kept going, not sure how, not sure why, the blood pouring down your face, your head on fire, burning so bright and so hard that not even the rain could cool it off.

"AND YOU DON'T remember nothing else?" your father says. You've driven all over town, every street, every dirt road, every hollow there is to stumble across in Stuckley, West Virginia.

"Not till she dropped me off at the hospital."

"Dumb fucking move if ever there was one."

"I seem to remember I was puking blood by that point, talking all funny."

"Oh, you remember that. Sure."

"You're telling me, in all this time, you never talked to Gwen?"

"Like I told you three years back, that girl got gone."

You know Gwen. You love Gwen. This part of it is hard to take. There was Gwen in your car and Gwen in the cornstalks and Gwen in her mother's bed in the hour just before noon, naked and soft with tremors, and you watched a drop of sweat appear from her hairline and slide down the side of her neck as she snored against your shoulder blade and the top of her foot was pressed under the arch of yours and you watched her sleep, and you were so awake.

"So it's with her," you say.

"No," the old man says, a bit of anger creeping into his puppy-fur voice. "You called me. That night."

"I did?"

"Shit, boy. You called me from the pay phone outside the hospital."

"What'd I say?"

"You said, 'I hid it. It's safe. No one knows where but me.'"

"Wow," you say. "I said all that? Then what'd I say?"

The old man shakes his head. "Cops were pulling up by then, calling you motherfucker, telling you to drop the phone. You hung up."

The old man pulls up outside a low, redbrick building behind a tire dealership on Oak Street. He kills the engine and gets out of the car and you follow. The building is two stories. The businesses facing the street are a bail bondsman, a hardware store, a Chinese take-out place with greasy walls the color of an old dog's teeth, a hair salon called Girlfriend Hooked Me Up that's filled with black women. Around the back, past the whitewashed windows of what was once a dry cleaner, is a small black door with the words TRUE-LINE EFFICIENCY EXPERTS CORP. stenciled into the frosted glass.

The old man unlocks the door and leads you into a ten-by-ten room that smells of roast chicken and varnish. He pulls the string of a bare lightbulb and you look around at a floor strewn with envelopes and paper, the only piece of furniture a broken-down desk probably left behind by the previous tenant.

Your father crab-walks across the floor, picking up the envelopes that have come through the mail slot, kicking his way through the paper. You pick up one of the pieces of paper, read it:

Dear Sirs,

Please find enclosed my check for $50.00. I look forward to receiving the information packet we discussed as well as the sample test. I have enclosed a SASE to help facilitate this process. I hope to see you someday at the airport!

Sincerely,

Jackson A. Willis

You let it drop to the floor, pick up another one:

To Whom It May Concern:

Two months ago, I sent a money order in the amount of fifty dollars to your company in order that I may receive an information packet and sample test so that I could take the US government test and become a security handler and fulfill my patriotic duty against them al Qadas. I have not received my information packet as yet and no one answers when I call your phone. Please send me that information packet so I can get that job.

Yours truly,

Edwin Voeguarde
12 Hinckley Street
Youngstown, OH 33415

You drop this one to the floor too, watch your father sit on the corner of the desk and open his fresh pile of envelopes with a penknife. He reads some, pauses only long enough with others to shake the checks free and drop the rest to the floor.

You let yourself out, go to the Chinese place and buy a cup of Coke, go into the hardware store and buy a knife with a quick-flick hinge in the hasp, buy a couple of tubes of Krazy Glue, go back into your father's office.

"What're you selling this time?" you say.

"Airport security jobs," he says, still opening envelopes. "It's a booming market. Everyone wants in. Stop them bad guys before they get on the plane, make the papers, serve your country, and maybe be lucky enough to get posted near one of them Starbucks kiosks. Hell."

"How much you made?"

Your father shrugs even though you're certain he knows the figure right down to the last penny.

"I've done all right. Hell else am I going to do, back in this shit town for three months, waiting on you? 'Bout time to shut this down, though." He holds up a stack of about sixty checks. "Deposit these and cash out the account. First two months, though? I was getting a thousand, fifteen hundred checks a week. Thank the good Lord for being selective with the brain tissue, you know?"

"Why?" you say.

"Why what?"

"Why you been hanging around for three months?"

Your father looks up from the stack of checks, squints. "To prepare a proper welcome for you."

"A bottle of whiskey and a hooker who gives shitty head? That took you three months?"

Your father squints a little more and you see a shaft of gray between the two of you, not quite what you'd call light and it sure isn't the sun, just a shaft of air or atmosphere or something, swimming with motes, your father on the other side of it looking at you like he can't quite believe you're related.

After a minute or so, your father says, "Yeah."

YOUR FATHER TOLD you once you'd been born in New Jersey. Another time he said New Mexico. Then Idaho. Drunk as a skunk a few months before you got shot, he said, "No, no. I'll tell you the truth. You were born in Las Vegas. That's in Nevada."

You went on the Internet to look yourself up, never did find anything.

YOUR MOTHER DIED when you were seven. You've sat up occasionally and tried to picture her face. Some nights, you can't see her at all. Some nights, you'll get a quick glimpse of her eyes or her jawline, see her standing by the foot of her bed, rolling her stockings on, and suddenly she'll appear whole cloth, whole human, and you can smell her.

Most times, though, it's somewhere in between. You see a smile she gave you, and then she'll vanish. See a spatula she held, dripping with pancake batter, her eyes burning for some reason, her mouth an O, and then her face is gone and all you can see is the wallpaper. And the spatula.

You asked your father once why there were no pictures of her. Why hadn't he taken a picture of her? Just one lousy picture?

He said, "You think it'd bring her back? No, I mean, do you? Wow," he said and rubbed his chin. "Wouldn't that be cool."

You said, "Forget it."

"Maybe if we had a whole album of pictures?" your father said. "She'd like pop out from time to time, make us breakfast."

NOW THAT YOU'VE been in prison, there's documentation on you, but even they'd had to make it up, take your name on as much faith as you. You have no Social Security number or birth certificate, no passport. You've never held a job.

Gwen said to you once, "You don't have anyone to tell you who you are, so you don't *need* anyone to tell you. You just are who you are. You're beautiful."

And with Gwen, that was usually enough. You didn't need to be defined—by your father, your mother, by a place of birth, a name on a credit card, a driver's license, the upper-left corner of a check. As long as her definition of you was something she could live with, then you could too.

You find yourself standing in a Nebraska wheat field. You're seventeen years old. You learned to drive five years ago. You were in school once, for two months when you were eight, but you read well and you can multiply three-digit numbers in your head faster than a calculator, and you've seen the country with the old man. You've learned people aren't that smart. You've learned how to pull lottery ticket scams and asphalt paving scams and get free meals with a slight upturn of your brown eyes. You've learned that if you hold ten dollars in front of a stranger, he'll pay twenty to get his hands on it if you play him right. You've learned that every good lie is threaded with truth and every accepted truth leaks with lies.

You're seventeen years old in that wheat field. The night breeze smells of woodsmoke and feels like dry fingers as it lifts your bangs off your forehead. You remember everything about that night because it is the night you met Gwen. You are two years away from prison and you feel like someone has finally given you permission to live.

THIS IS WHAT few people know about Stuckley, West Virginia—every now and then, someone finds a diamond. They were in a plane that went down in a storm in '51, already blown well off course, flying a crate of Israeli stones down the eastern seaboard toward Miami. Plane went down in a coal mine, torched Shaft #3, took some swing-shift miners with it. The government showed up along with members of an international gem consortium, got the bodies out of there and went to work looking for the diamonds. Found most of them, or so they claimed, but for decades afterward there were rumors, given occasional credence by the sudden sight of a miner still grimed brown by the shafts, tooling around town in a Cadillac.

You'd been here peddling hurricane insurance in trailer parks when word got around that someone had found one as big as a casino chip. Miner by the name of George Brunda suddenly buying drinks, talking to his travel agent. You and Gwen shot pool with him one night, and you could see it in the bulges under his eyes, the way his laughter exploded—too high, too fast, gone chalky with fear.

He didn't have much time, old George, and he knew it, but he had a mother in a rest home, and he was making the arrangements to get her transferred. George was a fleshy guy, triple-chinned, and dreams he'd probably forgotten he'd ever had were rediscovered and weighted in his face, jangling and pulling the flesh.

"Probably hasn't been laid in twenty years," Gwen said when George went to the bathroom. "It's sad. Poor sad George. Never knew love."

Her pool stick pressed against your chest as she kissed you and you could taste the tequila, the salt, and the lime on her tongue.

"Never knew love," she whispered in your ear, an ache in the whisper.

"WHAT ABOUT THE fairground?" your father says as you leave the office of True-Line Efficiency Experts Corp. "Maybe you hid it there. You always had a fondness for that place."

You feel a small hitch. In your leg, let's say. Just a tiny clutching sensation in the back of your right calf, but you walk through it, and it goes away.

You say to your father as you reach the car. "You really drive her home this morning?"

"Who?"

"Mandy?"

"Who's . . . ?" Your father opens his door, looks at you over it. "Oh, the whore?"

"Yeah."

"Did I drive her home?"

"Yeah."

Your father pats the top of the door, his denim jacket flapping around his wrist, his eyes the blue of bullet casing. You feel, as you always have, reflected in them, even when you aren't, couldn't be, wouldn't be.

"Did I drive her home?" A smile bounces in the rubber of your father's face.

"Did you drive her home?" you say.

That smile's all over the place now, the eyebrows too. "Define home."

You say, "I wouldn't know, would I?"

"You're still pissed at me because I killed Fat Fuck."

"George."

"What?"

"His name was George."

"He would have ratted."

"To who? It wasn't like he could file a claim. Wasn't a fucking lottery ticket."

Your father shrugs, looks off down the street.

"I just want to know if you drove her home."

"I drove her home," your father says.

"Yeah?"

"Oh, sure."

"Where'd she live?"

"Home," he says and gets behind the wheel, starts the ignition.

YOU NEVER FIGURED George Brunda for smart, and it was only after a full day in his house, going through everything down to the point of removing the drywall and putting it back, touching up the paint, resealing it, that Gwen said:

"Where's the mother stay again?"

That took uniforms, Gwen as a nurse, you as an orderly, Gentleman Pete out in the car while your father kept watch on George's mine adit and monitored police activity over a scanner.

The old lady said, "You're new here and quite pretty," as Gwen shot her up with phenobarbital and Valium and you went to work on the room.

This was the glitch—you'd watched George drive to work; watched him enter the mine. No one saw him come back out again, because no one was looking on the other side of the hill, the exit of a completely different shaft. So while your father watched the front, George took off out the back, drove over to check on his investment, walked in the room just as you pulled the rock from the back of the mother's radio, George looking politely surprised, as if he'd stepped into the wrong room.

He smiled at you and Gwen, held up a hand in apology, and backed out of the room.

Gwen looked at the door, looked at you.

You looked at Gwen, looked at the window, looked at the rock filling the center of your palm, the entire center of your palm.

Looked at the door.

Gwen said, "Maybe we—"

And George came through the door again, nothing polite in his face, a gun in his hand. And not any regular gun, a motherfucking six-shooter, like they carried in westerns, long, thin barrel, a family heirloom maybe, passed down from a great-great-great-grandfather, not even a trigger guard, just the trigger, and crazy fat fucking George the lonely unloved pulling back on it and squeezing off two rounds, the first of which went out the window, the second of which hit metal somewhere in the room and then bounced off that and then the old lady went, "Ooof," even though she was doped up and passed out, and it sounded to you like she'd eaten something that didn't agree with her. You could picture her sitting in a restaurant, halfway through coffee, placing a hand to her belly, saying it: "Ooof." And George would come around to her chair, say, "Is everything okay, Mama?"

But he wasn't doing that now, because the old lady went ass-over-teakettle out of the bed and hit the floor and George dropped the gun and stared at her and said, "You shot my mother."

And you said, "*You* shot your mother," your entire body jetting sweat through the pores all at once.

"No, you did. No, you did."

You said, "Who was holding the fucking gun?"

But George didn't hear you. George jogged three steps and dropped to his knees. The old lady was on her side, and you could see the blood, not much of it, staining the back of her white johnny.

George cradled her face, looked into it, and said, "Mother. Oh, Mother, oh, Mother, oh, Mother."

And you and Gwen ran right the fuck out of that room.

IN THE CAR, Gwen said, "You saw it, right? He shot his own mother in the ass."

"He did?"

"He did," she said. "Baby, she's not going to die from that."

"Maybe. She's old."

"She's old, yeah. The fall from the bed was worse."

"We shot an old lady."

"We didn't shoot her."

"In the ass."

"We didn't shoot anyone. He had the gun."

"That's how it'll play, though. You know that. An old lady. Christ."

Gwen's eyes the size of that diamond as she looked at you and then she said, "Ooof."

"Don't start," you said.

"I can't help it. Bobby, Jesus."

She said your name. That's your name—Bobby. You loved hearing her say it.

Sirens coming up the road behind you now and you're looking at her and thinking this isn't funny, it isn't, it's fucking sad, that poor old lady, and thinking, Okay, it's sad, but God, Gwen, I will never, ever live without you. I just can't imagine it anymore. I want to . . . What?

And the wind is pouring into the car, and the sirens are growing louder and there are several of them, an army of them, and Gwen's face is an inch from yours, her hair falling from behind her ear and whipping across her mouth, and she's looking at you, she's seeing you—really *seeing* you; nobody'd ever done that; nobody—tuned to you like a radio tower out on the edge of the unbroken fields of wheat, blinking red under a dark blue sky, and that night breeze lifting your bangs was her, for Christ's sake, her, and she's laughing, her hair in her teeth, laughing because the old lady had fallen out of bed and it isn't funny, it isn't and you'd said the first part in your head, the "I want to" part, but you say the second part aloud:

"Dissolve into you."

And Gentleman Pete, up there at the wheel, on this dark country road, says, "What?"

But Gwen says, "I know, baby. I know." And her voice breaks around the words, breaks in the middle of her laughter and her fear and her guilt and she takes your face in her hands as Pete drives up on the interstate and you see all those siren lights washing across the back window like Fourth of July ice cream and then the window comes down like yanked netting and chucks glass pebbles into your shirt and you feel something in your head go all shifty and loose and hot as a cigarette coal.

THE FAIRGROUND IS empty and you and your father walk around for a bit. The tarps over some of the booths have come undone at the corners, and they rustle and flap, caught between the wind and the wood, and your father watches you, waiting for you to remember, and you say, "It's coming back to me. A little."

Your father says, "Yeah?"

You hold up your hand, tip it from side to side.

Out behind the cages where, in summer, they set up the dunking machine and the bearded lady's chair and the fast-pitch machines, you see a fresh square of dirt, recently tilled, and you stand over it until your old man stops beside you and you say, "Mandy?"

The old man chuckles softly, scuffs at the dirt with his shoe, looks off at the horizon.

"I held it in my hand, you know," you say.

"I'd figure," the old man says.

It's quiet, the land flat and metal-blue and empty for miles in every direction, and you can hear the rustle of the tarps and nothing else, and you know that the old man has brought you here to kill you. Picked you up from prison to kill you. Brought you into the world, probably, so eventually he could kill you.

"Covered the center of my palm."

"Big, huh?"

"Big enough."

"Running out of patience, boy," your father says.

You nod. "I'd guess you would be."

"Never my strong suit."

"No."

"This has been nice," your father says and sniffs the air. "Like old times, reconnecting and shit."

"I told her that night to just go, just get, just put as much country as she could between you and her until I got out. I told her to trust no one. I told her you'd stay hot on her trail even when all logic said you'd quit. I told her even if I told you I had it, you'd have to cover your bets—you'd have to come looking for her."

Your father looks at his watch, looks off at the sky again.

"I told her if you ever caught up to her to take you to the fairgrounds."

"Who's this we're talking about?"

"Gwen." Saying her name to the air, to the flapping tarps, to the cold.

"You don't say." Your father's gun comes out now. He taps it against his outer knee.

"Told her to tell you that's all she knew. I'd hid it here. Somewhere here."

"Lotta ground."

You nod.

Your father turns so you are facing, his hands crossed over his groin, the gun there, waiting.

"The kinda money that stone'll bring," your father says, "a man could retire."

"To what?" you say.

"Mexico."

"To what, though?" you say. "Mean old man like you? What else you got, you ain't stealing something, killing somebody, making sure no one alive has a good fucking day?"

The old man shrugs, and you watch his brain go to work, something bugging him finally, something he hasn't considered until now.

"It just come to me," he says, his eyes narrowing as they focus on yours.

"What's that?"

"You've known for, what, three years now that Gwen is no more?"

"Dead."

"If you like," your father says. "Dead."

"Yeah."

"Three years," your father says. "Lotta time to think."

You nod.

"Plan."

You give him another nod.

Your father looks down at the gun in his hand. "This going to fire?"

You shake your head.

Your father says, "It's loaded. I can feel the mag weight."

"Jack the slide," you say.

He gives it a few seconds, then tries. He yanks back hard, bending over a bit, but nothing. The slide is stone.

"Krazy Glue," you say. "Filled the barrel too."

You pull your hand from your pocket, open up the knife. You're very talented with a knife. Your father knows this. He's seen you win money this way, throwing knives at targets, dancing blades between your fingers in a blur.

You say, "Wherever you buried her, you're digging her out."

The old man nods. "I got a shovel in the trunk."

You shake your head. "With your hands."

DAWN IS COMING up, the sky bronzed with it along the lower reaches, when you let the old man use the shovel. His nails are gone, blood crusted black all over the older cuts, red seeping out of the newer ones. The old man broke down crying once. Another time, he got mean, told you you aren't his anyway, some whore's kid he found in a barrel, decided might come in useful on a missing-baby scam they were running back then.

You say, "Was this in Las Vegas? Or Idaho?"

When the shovel hits bone, you say, "Toss it back up here," and step back as the old man throws the shovel out of the grave.

The sun is up now and you watch the old man claw away the dirt for a while and then there she is, all black and rotted, bones exposed in some places, her rib cage reminding you of the scales of a large fish you saw dead on a beach once in Oregon.

The old man says, "Now, what?" and tears flee his eyes and drip off his chin.

"What'd you do with her clothes?"

"Burned 'em."

"I mean, why'd you take 'em off in the first place?"

The old man looks back at the bones, says nothing.

"Look closer," you say. "Where her stomach used to be."

The old man squats, peering, and you pick up the shovel.

Until Gwen, you had no idea who you were. None. During Gwen, you knew. After Gwen, you're back to wondering.

You wait. The old man keeps cocking and recocking his head to get a better angle, and finally, finally, he sees it.

"Well," he says, "I'll be damned."

You hit him in the head with the shovel, and the old man says, "Now, hold on," and you hit him again, seeing her face, the mole on her left breast, her laughing once with her mouth full of popcorn, and then the third swing makes the old man's head tilt funny on his neck, and you swing once more to be sure and then sit down, feet dangling into the grave.

You look at the blackened shriveled thing lying below your father and you see her face with the wind coming through the car and her hair in her teeth and her eyes seeing you and taking you into her like food, like blood, like what she needed to breathe, and you say, "I wish . . ." and sit there for a long time with the sun beginning to warm the ground and warm your back and the breeze returning to make those tarps flutter again, desperate and soft.

"I wish I'd taken your picture," you say finally. "Just once."

And you sit there until it's almost noon and weep for not protecting her and weep for not being able to know her ever again, and weep for not knowing what your real name is, because whatever it is or could have been is buried with her, beneath your father, beneath the dirt you begin throwing back in.

CORONADO

A Play in Two Acts

Introduction

I WROTE THE first draft of "Until Gwen" in a mad rush one night on my front porch in Boston. The porch is surrounded by a hundred-year-old wisteria. This proved crucial because a storm hit that night, a torrent of rain and lightning unlike any I'd ever seen before outside of the South. It was with that mad-scientist vibe, as the rain clattered on the roof and snapped off the street, that I wrote the first draft, from around seven in the evening until about four in the morning. I rewrote it a few times over the next few days and then shipped it off to Great Britain, to the writer John Harvey, who'd commissioned it for an anthology he was editing called *Men from Boys*. I went back to work on other things. But the story never quite let go. Bobby and Bobby's Father and poor Gwen kept walking around in my head, telling me that we weren't done yet, that there were more things to say about the entangled currents that made up their bloodlines and their fate.

AROUND THIS TIME my brother, Gerry, showed up at my house. Gerry's an actor in New York, and he arrived on my doorstep one Christmas Eve with two actress friends. The four of us spent the next ten days shooting pool in my basement, watching old movies, and talking about the nature of drama and story and the creative process. We also talked, usually around 3 or 4 A.M. in my kitchen, about the various lost loves and discarded hopes that accumulate as one's life progresses in all its noise and folly. It felt like college, or certainly my early twenties; several nights, joined by other friends, we even ended up sitting on the floor. During those ten days, we hatched the idea that I would finally write a role for my brother and a play for the theater company to which he belongs. An aspect of my brother, Gerry, that's worth mentioning—he is one of the nicest human beings I've ever known. In the top two, actually. The problem is that this innate decency often leads him to be typecast in "nice guy" roles. I promised him I would create his role against type: I would write him the meanest, nastiest, most unconscionable monster I could imagine.

FINDING THAT MONSTER proved surprisingly easy because I'd already written him: Bobby's Father. I've created villains before, but most are tortured or misunderstood and a lot less villainous than we might prefer in terms of our comfort level with the human race as a whole. Bobby's Father, however, is all-villain-all-the-time. He possesses some measure of charm (I hope) that might make him a fun bar companion on a slow night, but otherwise he's irredeemable. So I started with him and that led me back to Bobby and Gwen. It also led me back to those kitchen conversations about love and loss and hope. Gradually other characters began to emerge—a psychiatrist and his patient, two lovers carrying on an illicit affair, a sad-sack husband, a comic-relief waitress. I had no idea who these people were or how they connected to the story I'd told in "Until Gwen," but every now and then one of them would mention a town called Coronado in such a way that suggested a measure of relevance, and I trusted these new characters would begin to account for themselves.

THEY DID. *HOW* they did is the point of the play. And if Gwen and Bobby and Bobby's Father never quite reach Coronado, and maybe none of the characters in any of my stories do either, then that's okay, I think. It's the trying that matters. The hope.

Coronado premiered on November 30, 2005, at Manhattan Theatre Source in Greenwich Village. It was produced and performed by the Invisible City Theatre Company, under the direction of David Epstein, with the following cast:

GINA	Rebecca Miller
WILL	Lance Rubin
WAITRESS	Elizabeth Horn
PATIENT	Kathleen Wallace
DOCTOR	Jason MacDonald
BOBBY'S FATHER	Gerry Lehane
BOBBY	Avery Clark
HAL	Dan Patrick Brady
GWEN	Maggie Bell

Coronado was performed as part of the closing-night festivities of the Writers in Paradise Conference in St. Petersburg, Florida, on January 28, 2006. It was produced by American Stage Theatre Company and Eckerd College with set design by Scott Cooper. It was directed by Todd Olson with the following cast:

GINA	Nevada Caldwell
WILL	Steve Garland
WAITRESS	Megan Kirkpatrick
PATIENT	Julie Rowe
DOCTOR	Dan Bright
BOBBY'S FATHER	Tom Nowicki
BOBBY	Steve Malandro
HAL	Drew DeCaro
GWEN	Caitlin O'Grady
YOUNG WOMAN	Talia Hagerty
MAN	Kyle Flanagan

Characters

WILL — *a man in his twenties*

GINA — *a woman in her twenties*

DOCTOR — *a man in his late thirties*

PATIENT — *a woman in her mid-thirties*

BOBBY — *a man in his late teens, early twenties*

BOBBY'S FATHER — *a man in his mid-forties*

GWEN — *a woman nineteen years old*

HAL — *a man somewhere between forty and fifty-five*

WAITRESS — *a woman of indeterminate age*

A MAN and a YOUNG WOMAN

Settings

ACT I takes place in an unnamed bar at various times.

ACT II takes place at the fairgrounds, a parking lot, and the bar, at various times.

ACT I

Scene 1

A booth in a bar where a couple, GINA and WILL, sit.

GINA   So how was the trip?

WILL   Lotta two-light, three-bar towns. Hartow, Rangely, Coronado.

GINA   How is that place?

WILL   It's coming up, I gotta say. Might be nice someday.

GINA   So you're back.

WILL   And you're going.

GINA   Just for a week.

WILL   A week. Jesus.

GINA   We can do two weeks.

WILL   Without talking? Maybe. Without touching, though?

GINA   I could bite through my lip looking at you.

WILL   I could . . .

[GINA *looks over at the bar, then back at* WILL.]

GINA   This is what I remember—the first time you touched me. The first time you ever laid a finger on my flesh. You remember?

WILL   It was after work.

GINA   You smelled of Paco Rabanne.

WILL   You wore that blue blouse.

GINA   You said you hated your car. You said . . .

WILL   Yes?

GINA   No, you tell me.

WILL   Not fair.

GINA   Fair-schmair. And yes it is.

WILL   I said . . . I said . . .

GINA   You don't have a clue.

WILL   I said . . . I said, "If you were air, I'd never take another breath just to hold you in."

GINA   I always wondered if you heard that in a movie.

WILL   Nope. All mine.

GINA   Say it now.

WILL   I just did.

GINA   Not quoting. Say it for real.

[*Beat.*]

WILL   If you were air, I'd never take another breath just to hold you in.

GINA   Mmm. Good line. Came as a surprise.

WILL   To me too.

GINA   How is that?

WILL   I don't know. We never know what we're going to say, do we?

GINA   Sure we do. We say "I need a haircut," and "I'd like a Fiero," and "I want a shelf organizer." And "You look terrific," and "What's on at ten?"

WILL   Sounds so depressing.

GINA   Until you.

WILL   Until me . . .

GINA   I could say "What's on at ten?" to you and not feel existential dread.

WILL   Until you, I, Jesus, fuck, I, my god, I mean, do you know I look at you sometimes and I just want to fucking cry? To scream? I want to grab you and squeeze you until your bones shatter. Not really, but you know? I want to tell the whole world that I couldn't kiss you enough, lick you enough, fuck you enough. There is no enough with you.

GINA   You know, you know when you're inside me or when I just catch a look from you—you're at your desk, I'm at mine—or when I think of the way you looked by the side of the road trying to jack up the car? Saying, "Stop, Gina. Stop laughing"? I think, my god, this is my life? God gave me this? And I think how I could just spread you on a cracker and eat you whole.

WILL   I think, I think, I swear to Christ, how my whole life I felt something missing, you know? Like you were out there, somewhere, and I knew it, I did, but I never found you so I finally stopped looking. I told myself it was a fantasy. A child's dream. Time to wake up, Will. So I did. I stopped believing and I got on with my life. I got on with my life. But then we met. And we talked. And suddenly I knew what I'd always known but tried to convince myself I didn't.

GINA   What?

WILL   That you were the piece of me that went floating off into the ether when they pulled me from the womb. And I'm, right, I'm barely a fetus but I'm reaching for you, going, "Hey, come back. Please." But you're gone. You're gone.

GINA   Oh God.

WILL   Oh Something.

GINA   And I think how since the first time you touched me on the . . . ?

WILL   Breast.

GINA   Chin.

WILL   Sorry.

GINA   Men. I thought, "Oh God, it all makes sense now. I can breathe. I can live. I'm, I'm home."

WILL   Home.

GINA   I'm home, Will.

WILL   Let's kill him.

GINA   Let's kill him.

WILL   Yeah.

GINA   Who?

WILL   Who.

GINA   My husband?

WILL   Yes.

GINA   Okay.

WILL   No, no really.

GINA   No, no really.

Scene 2

Another booth. The DOCTOR, *a psychiatrist, is meeting with his* PATIENT, *a woman.*

PATIENT   So, okay, we're here.

DOCTOR   We're here. At your insistence.

PATIENT   No, no. Yours.

DOCTOR   You asked to meet. I suggested a public place.

PATIENT   A bar. This bar.

DOCTOR   A public place.

PATIENT   With liquor.

DOCTOR   As opposed to a Wal-Mart?

PATIENT   As opposed to a Starbucks.

DOCTOR   I don't drink coffee.

PATIENT   Maybe you should take it up.

DOCTOR   I like tea. It's better for you.

PATIENT   And yet we're here. So's it safe to say you like liquor more than tea?

[DOCTOR *stands.* PATIENT *is oblivious.*]

PATIENT [*cont'd*]   Can we assume that?

DOCTOR   I'm going.

[PATIENT *notices him standing.*]

PATIENT   Doctor, please.

DOCTOR   This was a bad idea.

PATIENT   Please.

[DOCTOR *places some money on the table.*]

DOCTOR   A terrible idea.

PATIENT   Just listen.

DOCTOR   There's enough there to pay for the drinks.

PATIENT   Just please listen.

DOCTOR   It was unprofessional of me. A bad, bad idea.

PATIENT   I keep . . .

DOCTOR   Please don't drink too much—

PATIENT   I can't . . .

DOCTOR   —if you drove.

PATIENT   I used to . . .

DOCTOR   Even if you didn't.

PATIENT   I used to remember things.

DOCTOR   There's a cabstand not too far. In front of that motel.

PATIENT   I forget birthdays I had. Parts of high school, college, my twenties, last year.

DOCTOR   Because you drink.

PATIENT   You're the one who wanted to meet here!

DOCTOR   And why? Why do you think that is?

PATIENT   Because you're projecting?

DOCTOR   Nice try.

PATIENT   I thought you were leaving.

[*He starts to walk.*]

PATIENT [*cont'd*]   I know where you live.

DOCTOR [*Stops, looks back.*]   I moved.

PATIENT   Two-twenty-four Stellar Lakes Lane.

[*Beat.*]

　　　　　Oh, I'm sorry—another round?

[*He slides into the booth.*]

Scene 3

Another booth. BOBBY *and* BOBBY'S FATHER.

BOBBY'S FATHER   So how was she?

BOBBY   I sent her home.

BOBBY'S FATHER   Before or after?

BOBBY   During.

BOBBY'S FATHER   How do you send a whore home during?

BOBBY   She kept interrupting the blow job to pontificate on the merits of Michael Bay films.

BOBBY'S FATHER   Who's that?

BOBBY   Movie director. Makes all those shitty movies like *The Rock* and *Pearl Harbor* and *Bad Boys.*

BOBBY'S FATHER   I like those movies. They've got clarity.

BOBBY   Clarity.

BOBBY'S FATHER   Yeah. No one's all confused about how they feel or what they want or any of that whiny-ass bullshit. They want to fuck the blond chick, they feel like blowing shit up. It's pure. So you sent her home.

BOBBY   I gave her cab fare.

BOBBY'S FATHER   She didn't use it.

BOBBY   Huh?

BOBBY'S FATHER   She came over to my room.

BOBBY   Your room.

BOBBY'S FATHER   Somebody had to prop her ego up, poor girl like that.

[*They stare at each other.*]

BOBBY   So what'd you do after?

BOBBY'S FATHER   I rinsed my dick in the sink and drove her home.

BOBBY   You drove her home.

BOBBY'S FATHER   I'm speaking Czech?

BOBBY   People do have a way of disappearing in your company, Daddy. You drove her home.

BOBBY'S FATHER   I drove her home. Yes.

BOBBY   Where'd she live?

BOBBY'S FATHER   Home.

[*Beat.*]

>   So what was it like?

BOBBY   You've never been?

BOBBY'S FATHER   Been in county a couple times, but the big house? No, no, boy, not for your old man. So tell me, come on.

BOBBY   It was like prison, Dad. The hard cons say you only do two days in prison. The day—

BOBBY'S FATHER   That right?

BOBBY   —you go in and the day you get out. I did the day they transferred me from the hospital ward and the day you picked me up in a stolen car with a hooker in the backseat.

BOBBY'S FATHER   And a bottle of Beam, don't forget.

BOBBY   And a bottle of Beam, thank you.

BOBBY'S FATHER   And some coke. That too.

BOBBY   That too.

BOBBY'S FATHER   So how's the memory?

[BOBBY *laughs.*]

BOBBY'S FATHER [*cont'd*]   What?

BOBBY   "How's the memory." I took two bullets to the head, old man.

BOBBY'S FATHER   I thought one glanced off.

BOBBY   Two bullets hit your fucking head, you don't get hung up on specifics.

BOBBY'S FATHER   That how it works?

Scene 4

GINA and WILL stare at each other. Gina's husband, HAL, approaches with a pitcher of beer in one hand, three shots in the other, and three beer glasses dangling from his fingers.

GINA [*Eyes still on WILL.*]   Hi, honey.

HAL   Little help?

[*WILL helps him place the pitcher and glasses on the table.*]

WILL   There you go, boss.

HAL   Mighty white of you, I must say. Many times as I've been in here, you'd think I'd have some suck with the bartenders. Nope. I wait like everyone else.

GINA   Lost in a sea of the great unwashed. Poor baby.

[*HAL sits beside her, begins pouring beers.*]

HAL   It's a trial. Lucky I'm such a sweetheart. So you took care of that Coronado thing?

WILL   Wrapped it up this morning. Came back as soon as humanly possible.

HAL   Now there's a sense of industry. I'll drink to that.

[*HAL and GINA and WILL throw back their shots.*]

HAL [*cont'd*]   I always told you, honey. Didn't I always say?

GINA   You always said.

HAL   In-dustrious. You okay?

GINA   Fine.

HAL   Sure?

GINA   Really. Yeah. Just tired.

HAL   Oh, I heard a good one today.

[*GINA lights a cigarette.*]

HAL [*cont'd*]   Do you have to?

GINA   Do you?

HAL   Fair enough. You smoke your cancer stick, I'll tell my joke. It's just I love her so much, you know, boy?

WILL   So the joke?

HAL   Oh, right. I heard this from Frank. You know Frank, right?

WILL   Frank in Shipping?

HAL   No. That's Frank Stebson. I'm talking about Frank in Accounts Receivable.

WILL   No. I don't know him.

HAL   Frank. Frank. You know the guy. Frank Corso. Big
            whale. Works in Accounts Receivable.

WILL   No.

HAL   Sure you do. Always doing *Saturday Night Live* rou-
            tines on Monday morning? Wears ties that play mu-
            sic? Frank. Funny as shit. He—

GINA   Doesn't seem he knows the man.

HAL   You don't?

WILL   'Fraid not.

HAL   Frank. From . . . Well, anyway, there's this guy who—

WILL   Is this Frank?

HAL   What? No. This is the joke.

WILL   My apologies.

HAL   Okay. Well, there's this old boy and he's got a son,
            kid's, you know, twenty-two or so, always loafing
            around the house. One day, the guy says to his son,
            "You need to get up on out this house and find your-
            self a wife cuz we about done feeding your ass." So
            the kid comes back about a week later, finds his father
            in the basement, says, "Daddy, I found me a woman."
            Father says, "Where she at, boy?" Son says, "Setting
            on the couch in the living room." So the father, he
            takes a stroll up there, then comes running back
            down to the basement. He says, "Boy, you can't marry

that girl. She's your sister, but your mama don't know it."

[*WAITRESS comes up to the table.*]

WAITRESS   You all right here?

WILL   Take another round, thanks.

[*WAITRESS nods and leaves.*]

HAL   So the son comes back a week later, the father's out in the shed. Boy says, "Daddy, I found me another woman." Father says, "Where she at?" Son goes, "Setting on the couch in the living room." Father goes into the house, takes a look, comes running back to the shed. "Son, you can't marry her either. She's your sister too. But your mama don't know it. So get rid of her." 'Bout a week later, the son's sitting in the house, sad and all, and his mama comes in, says, "What happened to those nice girls you were bringing around? I thought you were gonna marry one of them." Boy says, "But, Mama, Daddy said I couldn't cuz they was my sisters." The mother says, "What?" And the boy says, "That's what he said. He said you didn't know about it." The mother says, "Well, don't you worry, son, you marry whichever one you please, cause he ain't your daddy."

[*HAL laughs uproariously. WILL chuckles. GINA smokes. The WAITRESS returns, places their drinks on the table.*]

GINA   Keep 'em coming, okay?

Scene 5

DOCTOR and PATIENT.

DOCTOR   So you've been forgetting.

PATIENT   What's the missus think of the new digs?

DOCTOR   So you've been forgetting.

PATIENT   Go to Crate & Barrel, did you? Get the latest stemware?

DOCTOR   You've been forgetting.

PATIENT   A lot.

DOCTOR   What're you on?

PATIENT   Nothing but the shit you prescribed. What's it? Haldol. I had a dog once. Had him from the time I was four till I was sixteen. His name was BB and when you stuck your nose in his fur it smelled like cinnamon. Don't ask me why, but it did. And I can tell you how he didn't so much walk as trundle. Is that a word? He trundled and his butt sashayed like a French hooker's. I loved that dog. So how come I can't tell you what kind of dog he was?

DOCTOR   He was a mutt?

PATIENT   If he was a mutt, I'd tell you he was a mutt. I'd remember he had a mutt's face. But I can't see his face. I can't remember what he looked like.

DOCTOR   You can't see his face.

PATIENT   Twelve years of my life and I can't see his face. It's the noise, the noise, the noise, don't you think?

DOCTOR   What noise?

PATIENT   What noise? The fucking bells, the whistles, the plethora of fucking choices for fucking nothing. The fucking Coast or Irish Spring or Ivory Snow. The SUVs and handbags and coats and diet pills and fitness programs and everything new-and-fucking improved! And you buy it so it'll fill those places in you that never did fill, those places you carry around in you like extra lungs? It'll make you feel right, but you're not filled, you're not right. And then you wake up and you can't remember what your dog looked like. Jesus Christ.

DOCTOR   Take a breath.

PATIENT   I'm breathing. I didn't forget how to do that.

DOCTOR   Well, that's something.

PATIENT   Yeah, that's something. Who are you?

DOCTOR   What?

PATIENT   Kidding.

Scene 6

BOBBY and BOBBY'S FATHER.

BOBBY'S FATHER   So you didn't stash it at Gwen's house?

BOBBY   Not that I recall.

BOBBY'S FATHER   Think.

BOBBY   I've been thinking.

BOBBY'S FATHER   So you're sure it's not there.

BOBBY   I didn't say I'm sure. I said "Not that I recall."

BOBBY'S FATHER   Well, recall better.

BOBBY   Would that I could. Where's Gwen?

BOBBY'S FATHER   I told you two years ago, that girl got gone. No note, no nothing, just blew out of town. Forget her. Shit, you forgot everything else. Forget Gwen. Hear me? Forget Gwen. So where do you think it is?

BOBBY   Like a bulldog on a pork chop.

BOBBY'S FATHER   You've got to have some theories.

BOBBY   Where's Gwen?

BOBBY'S FATHER   Caracas. Uzbekistan. Kathmandu. I told you. I don't know.

BOBBY   So maybe it's with her.

BOBBY'S FATHER   No.

BOBBY   Why not?

BOBBY'S FATHER   You told me.

BOBBY   I did? What I tell you?

BOBBY'S FATHER   You called me from the hospital parking lot.

BOBBY   I did? The hospital? No shit?

BOBBY'S FATHER   Dumb fucking move if ever there was one, her dropping you there.

BOBBY   I seem to remember I was bleeding all over the place by that point, starting to talk all funny.

BOBBY'S FATHER   Oh, sure, you remember that.

BOBBY   So what'd I say when I called you?

BOBBY'S FATHER   You fucking with me?

BOBBY   Perish the thought.

BOBBY'S FATHER   Are you?

BOBBY   Just asking what I said.

BOBBY'S FATHER   You said, "I hid it somewhere safe. No one knows where but me."

BOBBY   I said all that? Wow. What else I say?

BOBBY'S FATHER   Nothing. Cops had pulled up by that point, were calling you motherfucker, telling you to drop the fucking phone and get on the fucking ground you fucking motherfucker. You hung up.

BOBBY   Cops do love saying "fuck." So I guess Gwen doesn't have it.

BOBBY'S FATHER   No, she doesn't.

BOBBY   Huh. Well, let's hope something jars my memory.

BOBBY'S FATHER   Yeah, let's.

Scene 7

The DOCTOR *sits alone in the booth. The table is littered with empty glasses. The* WAITRESS *approaches.*

WAITRESS   Let me get some of those out of your way, honey.

DOCTOR   Thanks.

WAITRESS   You guys want another?

DOCTOR   Sure. Why not?

[*The* WAITRESS *leaves as the* PATIENT *returns from the bathroom. She sits, looks across at him. They both laugh.*]

PATIENT   What?

DOCTOR   What, what?

PATIENT   You're lit.

DOCTOR   I am.

PATIENT   How unseemly of you.

DOCTOR   I hate those "un" words that have no correlative.

PATIENT   Big-word breakfast this morning?

DOCTOR   You know what I mean. You hear of someone being

un-seemly, but never seemly. No one says "His behavior was impeccably seemly." Or did you ever hear of someone being "kempt"? No really. You're always un-kempt. I'd like to be there, alive and ticking, the day someone says "This is Ted. He's kind to his mother, has perfect dental, drives an Audi, and is astonishingly kempt."

PATIENT   Wow. You are so lit.

DOCTOR   I am. It's pleasant.

[*WAITRESS returns with their drinks. She leaves.*]

PATIENT   Bit of a slippery slope we're on, Doctor, don't you think?

DOCTOR   What do you mean?

PATIENT   Weren't you the one who advised me against being coy? Who's coy now?

DOCTOR   Madam, I object to the imputation. I am not being coy, I am being drunk. And if the slippery slope to which you refer has an end point of illicit sexual congress, I can assure you that the liquor has made that far more of a moot point than a likely occurrence.

PATIENT   You're too drunk to get it up.

DOCTOR   Precisely.

PATIENT   Who's going to need a cab now?

DOCTOR   Cheers.

PATIENT   But won't the missus wonder where the car is in the morning? And why that car was left outside a honky-tonk in the unincorporated part of the county?

DOCTOR   Let's leave her out of this.

PATIENT   You leave her out of a lot, I'd bet. Is she pretty?

DOCTOR   Yes.

PATIENT   Smart?

DOCTOR   Very.

PATIENT   Don't-drink-don't-smoke-what-do-you-do kinda gal?

DOCTOR   I'm not trying to make it bad.

PATIENT   You're not trying to make it bad?

DOCTOR   I'm trying to make it good. I am.

PATIENT   Meeting me in a bar so you can fuck me, that's trying to make it good?

DOCTOR   I'm not trying to fuck you.

PATIENT   Yes, you are.

DOCTOR   No, I'm not.

PATIENT   Yes, you are.

DOCTOR   No, I'm—

PATIENT   This isn't your office. This isn't therapy. This is you trying to tap my ass in a fucking bar.

DOCTOR   No, no. I removed that from the table. You remember? I did. I said I was too drunk. I did.

PATIENT   Then why are you here?

DOCTOR   Because you called me.

PATIENT   So?

DOCTOR   So?

PATIENT   So?

DOCTOR   Grace, I—

PATIENT   My name's not Grace.

DOCTOR   Your name's not . . . ?

PATIENT   My name's not Grace. Close, but no Ci-Grace.

Scene 8

BOBBY and BOBBY'S FATHER settle into a booth.

BOBBY'S FATHER   Well, that was utterly fucking fruitless.

BOBBY   I got some glue.

BOBBY'S FATHER   Gives me such a warm feeling inside. Where
           is it?

BOBBY   Right here.

[*BOBBY produces a tube of Krazy Glue. He applies some to the ash-
tray, then affixes a coin to it.*]

BOBBY'S FATHER   No, I meant—

BOBBY   Shit's amazing. You could glue a monkey's ass to a guy's
           head and it would never come off. The guy's stuck with

it, the monkey shitting all over his head, and he'd have to feed it, I guess, but that monkey's just banging away on the guy's face and the guy can't do a fucking thing short of scalping himself or that monkey's there for life.

BOBBY'S FATHER   Fuck the glue. Where is it?

BOBBY   Beats me.

BOBBY'S FATHER   The memory, right.

BOBBY   It's a tricky thing.

BOBBY'S FATHER   Sure, sure. Common problem—people misplacing a three-million-dollar diamond.

BOBBY   You misplaced a wife.

BOBBY'S FATHER   She misplaced me. Then she died.

BOBBY   The two events entirely unrelated I'm sure.

[BOBBY'S FATHER *reaches out and grips* BOBBY'S *ear.*]

BOBBY'S FATHER   We're not going to have this conversation again. Hear? Now where's the fucking diamond?

[*Beat.*]

You think blood'll save you?

BOBBY   Who's it ever saved?

BOBBY'S FATHER   Oh, well, now . . . a lot of shitty princes, a few useless princesses would have been ass-fucked and toothless 'fore they were twelve else-wise.

BOBBY   Outside of royalty. Who's it ever saved, Daddy? You?

BOBBY'S FATHER   Your ear's getting all sweaty.

BOBBY   Give it back.

BOBBY'S FATHER   But it's mine.

BOBBY   We'll call it a loan.

[*BOBBY'S FATHER smiles, lets go of his ear.*]

Scene 9

DOCTOR and PATIENT.

DOCTOR   You lied to me.

PATIENT   You fucked me.

DOCTOR   We fucked. Let's be plain. Okay? Let's be plain. We
           fucked. Once. A mistake I've admitted to repeatedly. I
           then referred you to another psychiatrist who special-
           izes in the very same.

PATIENT   The very same.

DOCTOR   Patients who have developed sexual and/or emotional
           attachments to their therapists.

PATIENT   And/or?

DOCTOR   Look—Grace or no Grace—we fucked.

PATIENT   Let's be plain—you fucked me.

DOCTOR   We fucked.

PATIENT   You fucked me.

DOCTOR   We fucked.

PATIENT   I know you are, but what am I?

DOCTOR   I—

PATIENT   What?

DOCTOR   I—

PATIENT   What?

DOCTOR   You shouldn't have told me you abetted in a murder, Grace.

PATIENT   That's your out? You slid your dick up and down and up and down and up—

DOCTOR   I know, I know.

PATIENT   —and down my clitoris. You remember that? And that was before you entered me. That was before.

DOCTOR   I know. But.

PATIENT   "But." Christ, you worked it like a wand and I came—

DOCTOR   Stop.

PATIENT   —twice—twice—before you even entered me. So, I dunno, what was that on your part? Confusion?

DOCTOR   You told me, you told me . . .

PATIENT   What'd I tell you?

DOCTOR   You told me—after—as we were lying together, and only then, that you'd helped someone commit murder. Nine months of therapy? Not a fucking word.

PATIENT   Sure, but I'd never had your cock in my mouth before.

DOCTOR   What—what—what does that have to do with anything?

PATIENT   You ever had a cock in your mouth, Stephen?

DOCTOR   No.

PATIENT   Well, then . . .

DOCTOR   You abetted murder. That's a capital crime.

PATIENT   I've done worse.

DOCTOR   You've . . . ?

PATIENT   I'll bet there're people everywhere—right now, right here in this bar tonight—who've done a whole lot fucking worse.

Scene 10

WILL, in a booth, chats up the WAITRESS.

WILL   I have no idea. Really.

WAITRESS   Well, he gave me the ring.

WILL   Sure.

WAITRESS   But he said hang it around my neck.

WILL   Exactly.

WAITRESS   From a chain.

WILL   And that's not the same.

WAITRESS   You don't think?

WILL   You don't.

WAITRESS   No, I don't. You're right.

WILL   I mean, I dunno. It could mean something real significant for him. But guys, you know?

WAITRESS   Exactly. Guys. But you're a guy.

WILL   Well, okay, I guess. I'm a—

WAITRESS   Right. You're a man.

WILL   I try.

WAITRESS   I was so sorry to hear about . . .

WILL   I know, right? Jesus. Who would have thought? I mean, you think of all the ways you could go . . .

WAITRESS   A train?

WILL   A train. You believe that shit?

WAITRESS   I've passed out in some weird places, though, so there but for the grace of god, I guess.

WILL   That's the thing of it, though. What's he doing down by the fairgrounds that time of night?

WAITRESS   It bugs you, huh?

WILL   And then to just stroll over to the train tracks and take a nap? Johnny Law accepts it, but it fucking pisses me off.

WAITRESS   You think . . . ? No.

WILL   And he's . . . I want all the *T*'s crossed and all the *I*'s dotted. You think that's too much to ask?

WAITRESS   No, no. And now she's . . .

WILL   What?

WAITRESS   Well, you know, the timing. They'd been planning it for so long and then it finally happens and he . . .

WILL   Dies.

WAITRESS   Oh god. What is she going to do?

WILL   I'll look after her. A man who wouldn't in these circumstances?

WAITRESS   I know. I know.

[*Notices* GINA *returning from the bathroom.*]

              You want another round, Will?

WILL   Sure.

WAITRESS   Should she be . . . ?

WILL   I dunno. But she is. Okay?

WAITRESS   Of course.

[*The* WAITRESS *waves her fingers at* GINA *and heads to the bar.* GINA *approaches the booth and she's obviously pregnant. She sits.*]

GINA   Flirting?

WILL   No.

GINA   I heard she's a hermaphrodite.

WILL   Hey, can you be gay and a hermaphrodite at the same
            time? Is that physically and emotionally and, well,
            gender-ly possible?

GINA   It's a question.

WILL   Hell of a question, I think.

GINA   Were you flirting with her?

WILL   Absolutely.

GINA   Really.

WILL   Can't flirt with you, can I? Bar's got eyes, babe.

[*The WAITRESS returns with their drinks, places them down.*]

WAITRESS   You feeling okay, honey?

GINA   Phenomenal.

[*The WAITRESS shoots WILL a look and then departs.*]

WILL   It's all okay.

GINA   No.

WILL   It is.

GINA   I don't think so.

WILL   What's different?

GINA   There's one less person in this booth for starters.

WILL   Yeah, I miss those jokes. You?

GINA   Don't do funny on this, okay? He's dead, Will.

WILL   Yes, he is.

GINA   And it doesn't seem to trouble you.

WILL   No, Gina, it doesn't.

GINA   How is that possible?

WILL   Eight hours sleep, proper diet?

GINA   You're clever. Clever and pretty-mouthed. Clever ain't enough.

WILL   You looked around? This is one dumb-ass county, honey. You want me to feel bad because Hal is dead. You want me to feel fear that we'll be caught. You want remorse. Doubt. I don't got any of that. Oops.

GINA   Bastard.

WILL   I want to reach out and hold your hands but I can't because everyone's watching. That hurts. Everything else, though? He's dead. He's gone. I can live with it.

GINA   You're energized by it. Reborn.

WILL   I'm born.

GINA   I'm nauseous.

WILL   Let's—

GINA   In the existential sense.

WILL   I still can't believe they taught Sartre at community college.

GINA   He's dead.

WILL   Yup.

GINA   Because of us.

WILL   Yup.

GINA   What will God say?

WILL   "Welcome to the club, don't park on the lawn."

GINA   Fuck you.

WILL   What's God going to say? "Gee, I was busy killing Indonesians in an earthquake and I hip-checked a few hundred thousand Africans with a sneak famine, but allow me to punish you for Hal."

GINA   You really don't.

WILL   Don't what?

GINA   Feel. Feel anything about this.

WILL   Life fucking goes on, Gina.

GINA   No. Don't you understand?

WILL   Yes. In your belly right now.

GINA   No.

WILL   In your womb.

GINA   It's all shit, Will. It's all stopped. The whole fucking clock. We killed a human being. We murdered. He might have told bad jokes and he might have been a racist and a sexist and a . . . a—

WILL   Douche bag?

GINA   But he was human. He had birthmarks and a mother who held him and a favorite smell and—

WILL   He liked to take long walks on the beach and his favorite color was blue and he cried whenever he watched *Brian's Song* and yet—and yet and yet—he's passed on. Like your grandparents, like your dog, like a friend who got colon cancer.

GINA   But we're why he's gone.

WILL   And I'm good with that.

GINA   I'm not.

WILL   You better get good, honey.

GINA   I—

WILL   You better get good. 'Kay?

GINA   You are—you're energized.

WILL   I'm the man who loves you. See that. Okay? I'm the man who loves you and lives for you.

GINA   I can't get it out of my head. The whole thing. I can't. Save me.

[*She reaches across the table toward him.*]

WILL   Not here.

Scene 11

BOBBY and BOBBY'S FATHER.

BOBBY'S FATHER   She's all you thought of in prison, I bet.

BOBBY   All I thought of since. All I thought of before.

BOBBY'S FATHER   I don't know where she got to.

BOBBY   I know that.

BOBBY'S FATHER   Do you?

BOBBY   But when you're seen—when you're seen—in this life, it's not natural to just let that go.

BOBBY'S FATHER   How you going to find her, though?

BOBBY   I just, I just, I think of her, I see her, I, and I say to myself, I say, "She's out there. Waiting."

BOBBY'S FATHER   She ain't waiting, son. She ain't. They don't wait. It's not their gift. That's why we love them. Because if we blink, they could be gone. We look right instead of left, they're already on a bus. Because they leave.

BOBBY   Not her.

BOBBY'S FATHER   Not her?

BOBBY   Not her.

BOBBY'S FATHER   Well, fuck her.

BOBBY   Already have.

BOBBY'S FATHER   You think anything's changed since we fucking cave-painted? They suck our dicks so we'll go to sleep. They share our beds so we'll keep them warm. They fuck us so we'll pay the electric. And if they suck our dicks and share our beds and fuck us just right, they know we'll buy them earrings and cars and fucking gym memberships. Because they can be alone, but they can't survive. And we can survive, but we can't stand to be alone. And that's it.

BOBBY   That's it?

BOBBY'S FATHER   We hunt, they eat. We build, they dwell. We produce, they use.

BOBBY   That's my inheritance, the sum of my received knowledge from you?

BOBBY'S FATHER   What did you think—you beat the house? You were the one guy in the history of time who found the perfect woman? You fucking infant. The free lunch ain't free, the check ain't in the mail, no one ever fought a war over truth or good intentions, and the only way not to lose is not to play.

BOBBY   More pearls. Thank you.

BOBBY'S FATHER   Where's my diamond?

BOBBY   Where's Gwen?

BOBBY'S FATHER   I told you.

BOBBY   Tell me again. Where's Gwen?

BOBBY'S FATHER   I—

BOBBY   Not good enough. Where's Gwen?

Scene 12

A slow song on the jukebox. PATIENT *lights a cigarette.*

DOCTOR   Those things will kill you.

PATIENT   You think?

DOCTOR   I never meant to—

PATIENT [*Waves it away.*]   No one ever means anything.

[PATIENT *stands, dances in front of him. He watches. She holds out her hand.*]

PATIENT [*cont'd*]   Come on. Dance with me.

DOCTOR   Don't be ridiculous.

PATIENT   I'm not being ridiculous. I'm being rhythmic. Come on. I'll even attempt to give a straight answer to a straight question.

DOCTOR   You will, huh?

PATIENT   Come on. I love this song.

[DOCTOR *stands and she pulls him out onto the floor. They dance, she much better at it than he.*]

DOCTOR   What's worse than murder?

PATIENT   What?

DOCTOR   You said you'd bet there are people in the world, in this bar, who have done far worse than murder. I'm wondering what that could be.

PATIENT   Did I say that? I must have been trying it out—the concept, the line. I do that sometimes. I don't mean anything by it.

DOCTOR   Sure you do.

PATIENT   After all your years climbing around in people's heads like a cranial janitor, do you think people know why they do things? People rationalize, they turn their delusions into something romantic that they can disguise as ethics or principles or ideals. People are selfish, Doctor—odiously, monstrously, but in so small and paltry a monstrousness that we barely notice it.

[*The* DOCTOR *tries to break away from her, but she grips him hard, grinds against him.*]

PATIENT [*cont'd*]   If we could have everything we wanted in an instant without fear of consequence? No worry of jail or societal reproof of any kind? No having to look our victims in the eyes because the victims have conveniently vanished? If we could have that? Stalin's crimes would pale in comparison to what we'd do in the name of love. In the name of the heart wanting what the heart wants. So don't fucking ask me what's worse than murder.

[*She drops his hand, steps away from him. Long beat.*]

DOCTOR   You're a sociopath. You are. And I'm leaving.

PATIENT   I will blow up your life.

DOCTOR   What?

PATIENT   You heard me. I will tell your wife and I'll tell the
Ethics Board and I'll tell the police and I'll make a
scene so loud the only place to put it will be the front
page. So don't you think of walking out of here, you
fucking theoretician.

Scene 13

BOBBY and BOBBY'S FATHER.

BOBBY'S FATHER   This memory of yours . . .

BOBBY   Yeah?

BOBBY'S FATHER   Well, it's a might selective, wouldn't you say?

BOBBY   If I could remember what it's being selective about,
I'd probably agree with you.

BOBBY'S FATHER   I'm just trying to think of what you've for-
getten besides, oh, the location of a three-million-
dollar stone. Seems like you remember every other
fucking thing.

BOBBY   Let's try your memory. Where was I born?

BOBBY'S FATHER   Not this shit again.

BOBBY   What's my mother's maiden name? Hell, what's her
             first name? Do I have a birth certificate?

BOBBY'S FATHER   I don't believe in paperwork.

BOBBY   Is Bobby even my real name?

BOBBY'S FATHER   It suffices. Look, your mother's dead.

BOBBY   So you say.

BOBBY'S FATHER   Why would I lie?

BOBBY   You've built your whole life on "Why would I tell the
             truth?" and you're asking me that? Let's start with an
             easy one. Where was I born?

BOBBY'S FATHER   New Mexico.

BOBBY   How hard was that?

BOBBY'S FATHER   No, wait, my bad. Actually it was New
             Orleans. I get the *New*s mixed up. I'm pretty sure it
             wasn't New Jersey, though. Where's my diamond?

BOBBY   New Hampshire.

BOBBY'S FATHER   Oh-ho. Now I'm seeing it.

BOBBY   It's sinking in finally, huh?

BOBBY'S FATHER   You were born here.

[BOBBY *sees the truth in his father's face.*]

BOBBY   This shitty little town?

BOBBY'S FATHER   This shitty little town.

BOBBY   So when we came here three years ago, you were, what?

BOBBY'S FATHER   Nothing. Scamming hurricane insurance in trailer parks, just like I said, just like we did. I ain't got no connection to this place no more. Just figured we'd pop in, as always, hit hard and fast and be gone. But you fall in luv, fuckhead.

BOBBY   And stumble across the diamond.

BOBBY'S FATHER   Yeah, that was a nice benny.

BOBBY [*Stunned.*]   Here?

BOBBY'S FATHER   Right here. Probably why you always get a woody for the fairgrounds.

[*BOBBY stiffens. BOBBY'S FATHER is oblivious, throwing back his drink.*]

BOBBY   The fairgrounds?

BOBBY'S FATHER   You always loved that place, right? Well, let me tell you something—makes me believe in genetic memory, boy, 'cause that's where you were probably conceived. Hey, that's an idea, maybe it's there.

BOBBY   The fairgrounds? Yeah, that sounds right.

BOBBY'S FATHER   What?

BOBBY   I said that sounds right. Want to go look?

[*BOBBY'S FATHER throws some bills on the table and stands.*]

BOBBY'S FATHER   I'll drive.

Scene 14

The DOCTOR *and the* PATIENT.

PATIENT   So I'm a sociopath.

DOCTOR   You have sociopathic tendencies.

PATIENT   You're parsing. I hate that. Have some balls. I either am something or I'm not.

DOCTOR   The human psyche can't be reduced to a simple this-or-that equation.

PATIENT   Sure it can. You, for example, are effete. A repulsive quality in anyone, but in a man? And like most people who are effete, you're pompous, and like most people who are pompous, you're insecure, and like all people who are self-consciously insecure, you make the rest of the world pay for your fucking insecurities. So if I have to choose between flaws, I'll take mine, thank you.

[DOCTOR'S *beeper goes off. He looks at the number.*]

PATIENT [*cont'd*]   The missus?

DOCTOR   I'll tell her I left it in the car.

PATIENT   How's the baby?

DOCTOR   Took his first steps last week. You hear about it, but you're never prepared for how . . . miraculous it seems.

PATIENT   I know.

DOCTOR   Oh, I didn't realize you were around long enough.

PATIENT   For what?

DOCTOR   To see your son take his first steps.

PATIENT   I wasn't. I watched from afar. They might not have been his first steps, but they were the first I saw him take.

DOCTOR   Are you finally ready to confront what leaving him did to you?

PATIENT   Is it true men are most likely to fool around on their wives in the first year after childbirth?

DOCTOR   Is that what happened to you?

PATIENT   That's what happened to you. To your wife. Why do you think that is?

DOCTOR   Because . . .

PATIENT   What?

DOCTOR   Because suddenly we're replaceable.

PATIENT   Let me tell you something—you're always replaceable.

DOCTOR   Suddenly we realize it. Men need to feel useful. Needed.

PATIENT   Yawn.

DOCTOR   I'm serious. Nothing makes you feel more . . . ancillary than seeing the love that used to be reserved for you transferred to a child.

PATIENT   Men need to feel worshipped. But once they have it, they get bored and go trolling for new parishioners.

DOCTOR   You reduce everything to a negation of honest emotion.

PATIENT   Who's rationalizing now? You put your dick in my mouth because you felt ancillary? Boo-hoo.

DOCTOR   I love my wife.

PATIENT   Ha!

DOCTOR   I love my wife. And I strayed, I failed. I did. But I love my wife. Hurts to hear, doesn't it? Because if one person can love—love deeply, if not flawlessly—then your belief that love is nothing but linguistic finery, well, it all goes up in smoke, doesn't it? And you're revealed as a fraud.

PATIENT   Ooooh. Doctor. My. Cutting to the quick, are we? I never said I didn't believe in love. I believe in love plenty. And no, my husband wasn't unfaithful after the baby was born. My husband was dead. My lover killed him.

Scene 15

GINA returns from the bathroom, settles into the booth. She is nine months pregnant. WILL is throwing back the Buds and shots of Jim Beam. They are silent for a long time.

WILL   We just don't talk anymore.

GINA   What do you want to talk about?

WILL   I's just fucking with you, baby. In a nice way.

GINA   I wasn't.

WILL   Oh god, here it comes.

GINA   Did you quit your job?

WILL   Who ratted?

GINA   You don't deny it.

WILL   No. I just want to know who ratted.

GINA   I might be on maternity leave but I still have friends.

WILL   Saved your life in 'Nam, did they?

GINA   Did you quit your job?

WILL   I already said I did.

GINA   Why didn't you tell me?

WILL   I'm telling you now, right?

GINA   Only because I asked. Only because I—

WILL   'Member when we used to have fun? You remember
          that?

GINA   I'm nine months pregnant. What do you want me to
          do—snort some blow and do it standing up against
          the chain-link fence?

WILL   I want a friend. A companion. Someone with balls and
          no fear of this bullshit life.

GINA   I'm pregnant.

WILL   That'll change. But you? Since Hal—

GINA   You promised you'd never say that name.

WILL   Fuck that. Since Hal, you're a wart. All sad and snif-
          fling and drag-ass bitchy. You're your mom. You're my
          mom. You're standing locked to the earth and letting
          it suck you dry instead of moving and telling the earth
          it ain't got no fucking title on you until it chases you
          down and swallows you.

GINA   There's no end to you. You never stop sucking.

WILL   We're here for a blink, baby. Father Time burps and
          clears his throat? We're over. And you want Barca-
          loungers from me? Fucking cookouts and layaway?
          We work our lives and save up just enough and get a
          time-share or some shit?

GINA   I'm wet.

WILL   Fucking mortgages and trade-ins and trips to the mall
          on Saturday? So—what—we can play by the rules and

still fucking die? That ain't going to be me. Take your fucking world. Take it. Let it suck you.

GINA   My legs are wet, Will.

WILL   It's a good speech, yeah? That's what I'm saying. We can go all Bonnie and Clyde and blow up this—

GINA   My water just broke, you moron.

WILL   "Moron" 's kinda harsh, don't you think?

GINA   Will.

WILL   All right, all right. What do we do?

GINA   Can you drive?

WILL   Fuck no.

GINA   Flag down your girlfriend and tell her to call the taxi.

[WILL *waves his arm wildly and the* WAITRESS *appears.*]

WILL   Call us a cab, V?

WAITRESS   Gonna leave that sweet new truck of yours in the parking lot?

WILL   Uh, V—

GINA   A fucking cab, please!

WAITRESS   Oh.

WILL   Yeah.

WAITRESS   Oh!

[*The* WAITRESS *bolts.* WILL *finishes his shot.*]

GINA   I am not having this baby with you.

WILL   Thank god, I was going to mention—I'm not into that
              delivery-room concept either. All the guck? I mean, I
              love you and all, but—

GINA   You will not be the father of this child.

WILL   A little late for that.

GINA   Yeah?

[*Slams the table in pain.*]

              I'm having this baby and you're fucking MOVING
              OUT.

WILL   We've had this discussion. You know how I feel about—

GINA   It's Hal's, you dumbshit.

[*The WAITRESS appears.*]

WAITRESS   It's on the way, guys. It's on the way. Hold on.

WILL [*Nods.*]   Kind of a private moment, V.

WAITRESS   Oh. We're all pulling for you all.

[*She runs off. WILL takes GINA's hand.*]

WILL   It ain't Hal's.

GINA   Your trip to Hartow and Rangely and Coronado, re-
              member? Our vacation after you got back? Do the
              math.

WILL   Ain't Hal's. Know how I know? Because it's mine. It's
              mine.

GINA   Have fun proving that, you shit. God! Get me to a
            fucking hospital!

WILL   [*Yanks her hand toward him.*]   Suck that pain up. Suck it
            up. You want to eat Cheetos on the couch watching
            Donahue the rest of your days and getting pig-fat,
            that's your prerogative. But don't you think—not for
            one fucking second—that you're taking my child.

GINA   I will cut your throat.

WILL   You wish.

GINA   I will.

WILL   That'd be great. Two dead lovers within a year. You
            get out of prison, the kid'll be—what—thirty-five?

GINA   Let me go.

WAITRESS [*Offstage.*]   Three minutes on the cab!

WILL   You'll drag your tired ass to some fucking trailer park
            and knock on the door and tell this adult that you're
            its momma. And it'll spit in your face. Killed both its
            daddies? Damn. What a piece of shit you are.

[*He lets go of her hand.*]

GINA   I will kill you.

WILL   Kill you first, bitch. You try and run. Just try.

GINA   I'll kill you, Will.

WAITRESS [*Offstage.*]   Dispatcher says "Two minutes!"

WILL   Make a deal?

GINA [*Screaming from the contractions.*]   Fucking deal? I'll—

WILL   Yeah, yeah. Kill me. I got that. Baby, look in my eyes.
            You wouldn't make the county line. Come on. Look in
            these baby blues. Look.

GINA [*Teeth clenched.*]   Your fucking deal?

WILL   Girl, it's yours.

GINA   I don't . . .

WILL   Girl, it's yours. Simple as that. You pop out an "X," go
            with god.

GINA   This is my child.

WILL   If it's a girl, it is. Can't mold no girl, that's for sure. But
            if it's a boy? Baby, I can show that child a world within
            the world that no one ever imagined. A true world.

WAITRESS [*Offstage.*]   We're down to seconds now, Will!

GINA   There's laws.

WILL   Not for me. You high? I will hunt you down. You
            know that. Ends of the earth, baby.

[*WILL proffers his hand. GINA clenches her fists, screams through
gritted teeth.*]

GINA   You'll never touch her?

WILL   You have my word.

GINA   Never see her.

WILL   Never.

GINA   Write? Nothing?

WILL   I never existed.

GINA   I would empty the gun.

WILL   And hit a barn. But whatever. If it's a boy, though?

GINA   I despise your breath. Your sweat. Your—

WILL   Shake my fucking hand, Gina.

WAITRESS [*Offstage.*] Taxi, Will!

GINA   I can't. I—

WILL   I don't know how to stop anymore. You know that. I don't know how.

WAITRESS [*Offstage.*] They're right over there!

GINA   If it's a girl you—

WILL   Disappear. Come on. Cab's here.

[*He grabs her hand. Shakes it. GINA looks at the hand.*]

ACT II

Scene 1

The fairgrounds. Night. BOBBY strolls with GWEN. In the background, the sounds of a carny in full summer swing.

GWEN   So tell me about her.

BOBBY   I can't remember her.

GWEN   Baby, everyone remembers their mama.

BOBBY   I can, a bit. Here and there. But there aren't any pictures.

GWEN   There's gotta be pictures.

BOBBY   If the old man ever took any, he burned 'em after she died.

GWEN   That's crazy. How could he not have taken one single picture?

BOBBY   He said, "You think it'd bring her back? No really, that'd be cool. Maybe if we had a whole stack of pictures, she'd pop up from time to time, make us breakfast."

GWEN   Your father did not say that.

BOBBY   He did.

GWEN   Even he can't be that cruel.

BOBBY   He can.

GWEN   Well, you're not cruel.

BOBBY   Never been tested. Hell, everyone's nice until some kind of hard choice is put in front of them.

GWEN   Bobby, I hate to break it to you, but you're good. You just are.

BOBBY   You're good. Jury's out on me. I mean, Christ, Gwen, I'm nineteen years old and I've been on the short con since I was six.

GWEN   You never conned me. You tried . . .

BOBBY   It worked.

GWEN   Only because I let it.

BOBBY   You say.

[*They kiss, a peck that turns into something longer.*]

GWEN   Owned your ass then. Own it now. Say it, bitch.

BOBBY   Never, never.

[*He lifts her and she slides her legs over his hips.*]

BOBBY [*cont'd*] You own me.

GWEN   You own me too.

BOBBY   Shit's about to get real serious.

GWEN   I know. I—

BOBBY   This is my old man we're talking about. My old man and money.

GWEN   Baby, how many times are we going to go over this?

BOBBY   As many times as we have to. Look, he thinks we're going to burn him. Because we'll be the first ones to touch that diamond. Shit, because on general principle he thinks everyone's out to burn him. Because he'd burn us if he had the chance.

GWEN   But we're not. We're—

BOBBY   That won't save us if anything goes wrong. If everything doesn't go exactly according to plan, he'll get it in his head that there was a double cross. He will. It's how he thinks. It's all he thinks. If this thing goes south, Gwen? Jesus.

GWEN   It won't.

BOBBY   So walk me through it.

GWEN   Bobby!

BOBBY   Come on. One more time. Baby, please. I got to know you can do it in your sleep.

GWEN [*Sits. By rote.*] Our best assumption is that poor, lonely George hid the diamond in his mother's room at the assisted-living place. But he still has to get out of town with it and his mother's been stuck in the home. But—lucky us—transportation date out of state set for . . . ?

BOBBY   Gwen.

GWEN   For . . . ?

BOBBY   Day after tomorrow.

GWEN   So we go in tomorrow in our spanking new nurse and orderly uniforms and find where he hid it.

BOBBY   Which entrance we use?

GWEN   Southeast rear.

BOBBY   That's the exit.

GWEN   Sorry, sorry. Northwest entrance, key code one-six-four-three. Up the north staircase to the third floor. Her room is first on the right through the door. Three-ten.

BOBBY   Nurses' station?

GWEN   Twenty-two yards to the left.

BOBBY   Janitor's closet?

GWEN   Directly across from Three-ten.

BOBBY   Security rounds?

GWEN   Ten-ten, ten-forty, eleven-ten.

BOBBY   Fire escape?

GWEN   To the right, end of the hall.

BOBBY   We run into a security guard?

GWEN   I rip my blouse, scream rape, and point at the guard.

BOBBY   Run into a nurse and a guard?

GWEN   Point at the nurse.

BOBBY   I'm laughing all the way to prison here. Laughing hard.

GWEN   Okay, okay. You take the security guard, I take the nurse, it's every robber for herself.

BOBBY   In the event we're split up?

GWEN   Rendezvous right here.

BOBBY   If I don't make it?

GWEN   Bobby.

BOBBY   If I don't make it, Gwen?

[GWEN *stares at him.*]

Scene 2

The fairgrounds. Night. The DOCTOR and the PATIENT.

PATIENT   Used to be a train ran past here. Route dried up, so they killed the service. Still see the tracks, though.

DOCTOR   It's too dark.

PATIENT   They're there. Dated a cop once. He drank so much I
          always figured he became a cop for the drinking. He
          told me once, swear to god, "Ever want to kill some-
          one, Gina? Do it with water or a train. Fucks the evi-
          dence all to hell." Irony, right?

DOCTOR   So your name's Gina.

PATIENT   According to the birth certificate, yes, sir.

DOCTOR   You killed your husband with a train.

[*Beat.*]

          He scream? He cry? Beg?

PATIENT   Not so much.

[*GINA, WILL, and HAL enter. HAL's arm is swung around WILL
and all three have been drinking. HAL's carrying a bottle.*]

HAL   It's fucked-up. I mean, I have kids from Number One.
          Now Number Two had no interest. She was nutrition-
          ally imbalanced anyway, so what the fuck. But Gina?
          Shit, boy, I never dared dream.

WILL   Well, boss, dreams have a way of coming true.

GINA   At a price, of course.

HAL   Ain't that the Bible truth? But, baby, trust me, ain't no
          price on this. You could leave my ass and take half my
          money and the beach house in Corpus, and I wouldn't
          care. Ha! Long as I had me a little shit kicker to kick
          shit with?

[*HAL sits suddenly. He laughs and hoots at the moon. GINA and WILL can't stop staring at him and then each other.*]

HAL [*cont'd*]   Yeah, a little tyke! A little tyke! Yee-hee. Got-damn!

DOCTOR   So . . . ?

PATIENT   I know. Right?

DOCTOR   But, you could have—

PATIENT   Oh, Doctor. Please. We are all—all of us—about the children.

Scene 3

Headlights cut across the fairgrounds. BOBBY and BOBBY'S FATHER exit their car offstage and enter the fairgrounds.

BOBBY'S FATHER   So we getting warm?

BOBBY   I'm feeling all tingly.

BOBBY'S FATHER   I always liked this place off-season, the tarps flapping in the wind, faint smell of elephant shit.

BOBBY   Ain't no elephants at a fair.

BOBBY'S FATHER   No?

BOBBY   You're thinking of the circus.

BOBBY'S FATHER   The circus. I hate trapeze artists. Women all look like men and the men all look like cock smokers. And don't even get me started on fucking clowns.

[*BOBBY stops at a freshly turned mound of dirt. He kicks it lightly with his foot.*]

BOBBY   Mandy?

BOBBY'S FATHER   Who the fuck's Mandy?

BOBBY   The hooker.

BOBBY'S FATHER   That was her name? Huh.

[*BOBBY kicks the mound again.*]

BOBBY   Oh, no, right, you drove her home. Which was where again?

[*BOBBY'S FATHER chuckles softly.*]

BOBBY'S FATHER   This has been nice, reconnecting and shit.

BOBBY   A time to treasure.

BOBBY'S FATHER   You think I'm shitting you, but I missed you, boy. I'm the only daddy you've ever known and you're the only son I've ever known and we had ourselves some times over the years.

BOBBY   Name one.

BOBBY'S FATHER   I could name a hundred.

BOBBY   Try one.

BOBBY'S FATHER   Why you gotta be cold?

BOBBY   I'm not being cold. I'm asking—

BOBBY'S FATHER   You'd a preferred going to some same-as-every-other-fucking-kid grade school? Playing video games in some stink-ass suburban basement? Some stink-ass suburban town with a mall looks like every other mall? You get through high school and go to college, study business or poli-sci? And then get you a job, a 401(k), marry the receptionist because she smiles at you right and gives okay head? And then you're thirty-five and she ain't giving any head anymore and you've got two kids crying for fucking video games and sneakers and your soul feels like a tomato left on a warm porch, but, wait, you got a couple pornos in the closet and a new fucking car and the supermarket's right down the street! So—hey—living large! And there's only fifty-five years to go if you live right, don't smoke or drink or eat food that tastes good, all so you can die in Florida in a nice white house while Guatemalans water your lawn. Hey, have at it.

BOBBY   You do like to spew, don't you?

BOBBY'S FATHER   You were born off the grid, raised off the grid, and lived off the grid. Shit, you don't even have a social.

BOBBY   They had to create it in county. Take my name on faith. Intake guard said he'd never seen anything like it. I didn't exist.

BOBBY'S FATHER   And ain't that fucking hot?

BOBBY   What if I wanted to be part of the grid?

BOBBY'S FATHER   Who wants that?

BOBBY   What if I wanted the choice?

BOBBY'S FATHER   Dang. I'm tearing up. Look.

[BOBBY *walks around, looking at the earth, cocking his head every now and then.*]

BOBBY   Yeah . . .

BOBBY'S FATHER   Yeah?

BOBBY   Sure. This could be the area.

BOBBY'S FATHER   It's really coming back now, huh?

BOBBY   Little bit.

BOBBY'S FATHER   'Cause I'm 'bout spent on patience.

BOBBY   I 'spect you would be.

BOBBY'S FATHER   Never my strong suit.

[BOBBY'S FATHER *produces a gun, taps it against his leg.*]

BOBBY   That supposed to help my recall?

BOBBY'S FATHER   Figured it might could hurry it up some.

BOBBY   Oh, you did?

Scene 4

GINA, WILL, and HAL in the positions we last saw them.

HAL You don't think I know, boy? Shit. My job is bullshit. I sit in a room every day just waiting to smell its lack. Its presence? I can smell that 'fore you even open the door.

WILL Boss, I'm being friendly here.

HAL I seen your friendly before. You think you're good because you grew up not wanting. Not wanting ain't good. It's just not poor. You ain't rich, but poor? That's evidentiary, son. That's experience. You ain't never had experience, so you only imagine you have a soul.

WILL I have a soul, boss.

HAL So you claim. Where the missus at?

GINA We're all drunk. Whyn't we just—

HAL Whyn't you just sit the fuck down?

[*HAL pulls out a pistol. GINA sits. WILL doesn't.*]

HAL [*cont'd*] Said, "Sit."

WILL Not going to do that, Hal.

HAL Sit.

WILL No.

GINA   Sit, Will.

WILL   Speak your piece, Hal.

HAL   Yeah. I's right about you, boy.

GINA   Jesus! You want me to measure them for you?

HAL   Will knows.

GINA   Knows fucking what?

HAL   Knows you never stop pedaling.

GINA   I'm drunk, but what'd you smoke?

HAL   You never stop pedaling. It's the law. Even if there's no one around to see, you never stop. 'Cause the moment you do? You ain't worth shit. No smiles from the salesmen, no "How do?'s" from the waitresses, no welcome woof from the dog. You stop pedaling? Hand that dick over, pick you out a satin pillow.

GINA   I don't know what you're talking about.

[*Lights up on the* DOCTOR *and the* PATIENT, *watching.*]

HAL   He does.

PATIENT   They never stop. They never fucking stop.

DOCTOR   Who?

WILL   Just making sure you don't drink too much, boss. Hope you'll be making that Coronado trip with me come Monday.

PATIENT   You. You. You. You fucking . . .

Scene 5

BOBBY and GWEN, exactly as they were.

BOBBY   If. I. Don't. Make. It. Gwen.

GWEN   It's ours, baby. Ours. Not yours. Not mine. Ours. And definitely not fucking his. I'm not just going to—

BOBBY   Yes, you are. He will never stop looking. Even when you're positive you've left no tracks. Even when all logic says he wouldn't, he couldn't? He'll still be looking.

GWEN   You've already told me this.

BOBBY   Did you fucking listen? You do not fuck around with this man. If anything happens to me, you get that diamond to him—by FedEx, by private courier, by Pony Express. I don't care, but you get it to him, and you don't deliver it in person, and still you run. You run till you're out of earth.

GWEN   He's a man, Bobby.

BOBBY   He's a lot less than that.

[*Puts his arm around her.*]

     You take naps, watch TV, read magazines. You daydream and make love and wonder what you're gonna wear and where you might be in ten years and if you'll ever have children. He doesn't. He lives to get. Robs to get. Wakes up to get. It's all he does. That makes him better at it than we'll ever be.

GWEN   Then he's nothing.

BOBBY   His nothing's a whole lot stronger than our something.

GWEN   Why not run now, baby?

BOBBY   Because we are going to burn him. Because I can accept losing to the prick, but not every fucking time. We're going to take our cut first before he can burn us. And then we'll send him his share from a state or two away. And we will fucking disappear, baby. Vanish.

GWEN   Did I mention you set my heart aflutter and make me feel all funny inside? How sometimes, like now, I just want to shove my hand in your jeans and—

[*BOBBY jerks away from her, but she rolls on top of him.*]

BOBBY   Hey. Witnesses.

GWEN   Where?

BOBBY   They could come.

GWEN   So could you, fool.

BOBBY   I'm serious, I'm serious. If it goes south, you bury it here and send him a postcard telling him how to find it. You don't get clever. You don't try to wrangle with him. You tell him it's here.

GWEN   I'll tell him it's here.

BOBBY   By then, it won't be our future. It'll be our noose. I'm serious.

GWEN   I'm serious.

BOBBY   Gwen.

GWEN   Gwen.

BOBBY   I am.

GWEN   I am.

[*She covers his face and body with her own.*]

Scene 6

HAL, WILL, and GINA.

HAL   Here's my thing.

WILL   What's your thing, boss?

HAL   I'm pedaled out.

WILL   You're a lying sack of shit.

HAL   I'm plumb done. I want to reach in that belly right now and pull out a whole baby and spend my final years raising it. I do. Let you—

[*HAL fires at WILL'S feet. WILL jumps back. GINA shrieks.*]

HAL [*cont'd*]   —run off together and take some of my property and a whole shitload a' my money. And that's fine. I just want to raise that child. Problem is, I can see your eyes, boy. And I know you can't abide that.

WILL   I might could.

HAL   Might could be full of shit.

WILL   The thing is? Hal? You say it now and maybe you feel
           it but you couldn't live it then. You'd try, I'll grant you.
           But one day, that kid's one or one and a half or four,
           and you'll get bored. Nothing else to do but watch it
           grow? Fuck, man. And then you'll need a goal. And
           you'll come after us. Because your pride and your
           fucking money won't allow you to take it.

HAL   You say. But, see, I just want to make someone safe.
           One person. My person, my child. That's a long-ass
           goal. And I'm going to hold its chubby legs and show
           it how to walk and keep it from biting into the exten-
           sion cords on the Christmas tree and walk it to school
           and—

[*GINA hits HAL in the head with the bottle. The train whistle blows.
GINA hits HAL again.*]

GINA   Fucking Christmas trees? You'll keep "IT" safe?
           What about me?

[*WILL grabs her, pulls her back.*]

WILL   Train's closing, honey. Ticktock.

Scene 7

BOBBY and BOBBY'S FATHER.

BOBBY   Held it in my hand, you know.

BOBBY'S FATHER   I assumed.

BOBBY   Filled the center of my palm. The whole center of my palm.

BOBBY'S FATHER   Big, huh?

BOBBY   Big enough.

BOBBY'S FATHER   Kinda money that stone'd bring? A man could retire.

BOBBY   To what?

BOBBY'S FATHER   Mexico.

BOBBY   To what, though? Mean old man like you? What you got if you ain't stealing something, killing somebody, making sure no one alive has a good fucking day?

BOBBY'S FATHER   It's the idea.

BOBBY   The idea.

BOBBY'S FATHER   Man needs a goal.

BOBBY   Uh-huh.

BOBBY'S FATHER   Getting awful bored now.

BOBBY   Heavens.

[*He points the gun at* BOBBY.]

BOBBY [*cont'd*]   Where's Gwen?

BOBBY'S FATHER   This is a real fucking gun.

BOBBY   This is a real fucking question. You want your rock? Where's Gwen?

BOBBY'S FATHER   You get taller in prison? I think you did. I'm pretty sure you grew an inch, maybe two.

BOBBY   I told her that night to just go, just get, just put as much country as she could between you and her until I got out. I told her even if I told you I had it, you'd have to cover your bets, you'd have to come looking for her.

BOBBY'S FATHER   Who's this we're talking about?

BOBBY   Gwen.

BOBBY'S FATHER   You don't say.

BOBBY   I told her if you did find her to tell you I'd only said one word about where I hid it.

BOBBY'S FATHER   And what word was that, pray tell?

BOBBY   Fairgrounds.

[BOBBY'S FATHER *smiles, taps the gun against his outer thigh.*]

BOBBY [*cont'd*]   Told her if you truly believed she didn't know anything you might—just might—show mercy for once.

BOBBY'S FATHER   And why would I do that?

BOBBY   Because I loved her.

BOBBY'S FATHER   Ain't no such thing.

BOBBY   You say! You say!

[BOBBY *takes a few steps toward him and he raises the gun again. The sight of it makes* BOBBY *laugh.*]

BOBBY [*cont'd*] Go ahead. Really. Pull that fucking trigger, tough guy.

Scene 8

GINA *and* WILL *drag* HAL *toward the train tracks, struggling with his weight.* HAL *comes back to consciousness but is still groggy as hell.*

HAL   Don't. Just don't. Just listen. I—

[WILL *shoves* HAL'*s gun under his chin.*]

WILL   Got your gun, Hal. Now shut the fuck up.

HAL [*Screaming.*] I'LL BE A GREAT FATHER THIS TIME, I WILL, AND GINA, I LOVE YOU, I DO, I KNOW I'VE HAD A FEW WIVES AND A BUNCH OF COCKTAIL WAITRESSES AND SOME STRIPPERS BUT NEVER ANYTHING LIKE YOU AND I'LL BE A GREAT DAD, A GREAT DAD, AND IF YOU COULD JUST SEE MY SOUL AND HOW MUCH I LOVE YOU, GINA, BABY, PLEASE, I—

[*They hurl* HAL *onto the train tracks. SOUND OF IMPACT.*

GINA *grabs her head and screams at the sky.*]

GINA   Oh my god oh my god oh my god oh my god oh my
            god . . .

[*WILL tucks the gun under his shirt, stares off.*]

WILL   Bye, Hal.

[*The DOCTOR and the PATIENT watch as the lights dim on WILL and GINA.*]

DOCTOR   You've confused your sins.

PATIENT   What?

DOCTOR   The hierarchy of them. You think you did something
            worse than murder? Leaving your child to be raised by
            Will? You had no choice.

PATIENT   I could have died fighting.

DOCTOR   End result would have been the same. You can't fight a
            guy like Will. You can't, Gina. The only thing that can
            stop a guy like Will is a guy like Will.

PATIENT   No, I—

DOCTOR   Your sin was killing Hal. You had choice there and you
            made the worst one. Do you even know why?

PATIENT   Because we were in love.

DOCTOR   You were in love. You could have divorced him. Was it
            his money?

PATIENT   Didn't hurt.

DOCTOR   He'd have given you that. So . . . Why'd you kill Hal,
            Gina?

Scene 9

BOBBY'S FATHER pointing the gun at BOBBY. [*Beat.*]

BOBBY'S FATHER   It just come to me.

BOBBY   Yeah, what's that?

BOBBY'S FATHER   You've known for, what, three years that Gwen is no more?

BOBBY   Dead.

BOBBY'S FATHER   Whatever.

BOBBY   Dead.

BOBBY'S FATHER   If you like. Dead.

BOBBY   Yeah, Daddy.

BOBBY'S FATHER   Three years. Lotta time to think.

[*BOBBY nods.*]

BOBBY'S FATHER [*cont'd*]   Plan.

[*Another nod. BOBBY'S FATHER looks at his gun.*]

BOBBY'S FATHER [*cont'd*]   This going to fire?

BOBBY   I'd say the odds are a might dubious.

BOBBY'S FATHER   It's loaded. I can feel the mag weight.

BOBBY   Jack the slide.

[BOBBY'S FATHER *yanks back hard. The slide is frozen.*]

BOBBY [*cont'd*]   Krazy Glue. Filled the barrel too.

BOBBY'S FATHER   Thought I felt a monkey on my head.

[BOBBY *produces a knife, expertly flips the blade free of the hasp.*]

BOBBY'S FATHER [*cont'd*]   The other great love of your life. I assume you've lost none of your talent with it.

BOBBY   Wherever you buried her, you're digging her out.

BOBBY'S FATHER   I got a shovel in the trunk.

BOBBY [*Shakes his head.*]   With your hands.

Scene 10

BOBBY *and* GWEN *sit in each other's arms at the fairgrounds.*

GWEN   You think it lasts?

BOBBY   What?

GWEN   This.

BOBBY   Of course. Why not?

GWEN   You look around, you see people who've been to-gether, I mean, do they look happy? How do you hold something that feels this good?

BOBBY   You just do.

GWEN   But it's got to burn after a while. It's got to exhaust
             you. Maybe you let it cool a bit, just a bit, so it lets you
             breathe normal again. But once you do that . . .

BOBBY   We don't need to breathe normal.

GWEN   Everyone needs to breathe normal.

BOBBY   We're not everyone.

GWEN   Yes, we are.

BOBBY   You're scared. Tomorrow's a scary day. But we'll get
             through.

GWEN   And then what? They never show you the ebb. I mean,
             it all ebbs.

BOBBY   And gathers steam and comes back again.

GWEN   You think?

BOBBY   I hope.

GWEN   I hope.

BOBBY   If it's pure . . . if it's pure, well, you hold on to what's
             pure about it. You never let that ebb. The other parts,
             okay, sure, they'll grow weak at times, but the pure part?

GWEN   We'll get old.

BOBBY   Fuckin' A!

GWEN   Fat. Cellulite. Wrinkles. No one will know we were
             beautiful once.

BOBBY   Speak for yourself.

GWEN   Bitch.

BOBBY   I can't wait to see each line in your face appear. To
          know I saw its birth.

GWEN   Where did you come from?

BOBBY   Pluto. You say I'm good. Well, I don't know about
          that. I don't. But we're good. I know that.

GWEN   I'm going to marry you, shithead. And get fat just to
          test your resolve.

BOBBY   Shave your head while you're at it, would you? I dig
          fat bald chicks.

Scene 11

*DOCTOR and PATIENT sit in exact same positions as BOBBY and
GWEN. PATIENT stares offstage at the sounds of the fair.*

DOCTOR   This is not remotely appropriate.

PATIENT   Let's not get into "appropriate" again. It's tired. I'm
          tired. Just let me sit here for another minute.

DOCTOR   Fair enough.

PATIENT   How do they do it? All those nobodies out there.
          Never Weres. Pass through this world, never achieve a
          single significant thing.

DOCTOR   Maybe their definition of "significant" is different.

PATIENT   What? Got a raise? Made VP of the Media Affairs

Department for Bo's Discount Furniture? Bought that power mower?

DOCTOR   Raised a child. Loved a parent. Died in her arms.

PATIENT   Hallmark bullshit. Lifetime Movie of the Week. The Noise we all tune in to so we won't see that we don't really matter. We left no mark. Those who are remembered offered a sacrifice.

DOCTOR   Everyone makes sacrifices in a relationship. It's part of—

PATIENT   A sacrifice made unto something. An offering thrown on a pyre so the gods know you're worthy.

DOCTOR   Of immortality? Happiness?

PATIENT   What adult believes in happiness?

DOCTOR   Then what?

PATIENT   Completion. The illusion that you exist for a purpose. You commit to, to true love—of a person, your art, your company, your country, your truth? When you feel that, you have to sacrifice something to it or else, else it's just infatuation.

DOCTOR   [*Points offstage at the fair.*]   That's why you killed a human being? So you wouldn't be them?

PATIENT   Yes. So I'd never, ever be them. And from then on, I had a secret that defined me as bigger than that. Better. More serious.

DOCTOR   And now?

PATIENT   Fuck you.

DOCTOR   And now?

PATIENT   Fuck you!

DOCTOR   AND NOW?

PATIENT   I want to undo it. I want to go back. I want my child. He's . . . he's eleven now. And he's out there somewhere. With him. With him.

Scene 12

BOBBY'S FATHER *has dug about four feet into the grave.* BOBBY *squats above him, watching.*

BOBBY'S FATHER   Come on. Let me use the shovel.

BOBBY   Tell me about my mother.

BOBBY'S FATHER   Let me use the shovel. I got no nails left, I got—

BOBBY   Tell me about her.

BOBBY'S FATHER [*Eyeing the knife.*]   Fuck you. You won't use that. You don't have the—

[BOBBY *stabs him in the shoulder.*]

BOBBY'S FATHER [*cont'd*]   Jesus!

[BOBBY *stabs him in the shoulder again.*]

BOBBY'S FATHER [*cont'd*]   All right! All right!

BOBBY   Tell me something about my mother and I might—might—give you the shovel for a bit.

BOBBY'S FATHER   You can't do this to me!

BOBBY   All evidence to the contrary.

BOBBY'S FATHER   I raised you.

BOBBY   A bit too well, I'd say. Have you ever loved anyone? Anything? I mean, tell me you had a dog as a kid. I'll buy it. A favorite uncle.

BOBBY'S FATHER   I loved you.

BOBBY   I was chattel. Big difference. Keep digging. I'm just wondering if I cut you open, if I'd find a heart. Or an engine.

BOBBY'S FATHER   Same engine that runs in you.

BOBBY   Did you ever love anyone?

BOBBY'S FATHER   I loved your mother.

BOBBY   What was her name?

BOBBY'S FATHER   Nope. That's mine, boy.

BOBBY   How'd you meet?

BOBBY'S FATHER   Give me some water.

[BOBBY *thinks about it, finally passes him a bottle.*]

BOBBY'S FATHER [*cont'd*]   I was a pencil pusher once. Believe

that? Regional manager for a grain outfit. Covered
sales for a five-state region. Had me a shitty car. Apartment wasn't bad, kinda nondescript, I guess you'd say.
Little patio looked out on a little pool and a bunch of
other patios. Thought one day I'd maybe run the show
when the old man retired. He was grooming me. Then
I met your mother.

BOBBY   What happened?

BOBBY'S FATHER   What didn't? The world shook. Never
looked the same after that. One day, we came out of
the building at the same time, started talking while we
walked to our cars. She had on this blue blouse . . .

[*He swigs some water, leans back against the grave. Beat.*]

BOBBY   That's it? The blue blouse? That's your fucking story?

BOBBY'S FATHER   You can't explain love. When it seizes you,
what it does. You end up sounding like an idiot. She
wore a blue blouse, we talked, I felt like God gave
birth to me that day. How about that shovel?

BOBBY   Is she dead?

BOBBY'S FATHER   She is to me.

[*BOBBY lowers his head for a moment. When he raises it, he wipes at
some tears.*]

BOBBY'S FATHER [*cont'd*]   Now you know.

BOBBY   Now I know. Climb out. Go get the shovel.

[BOBBY'S FATHER *climbs out, starts walking toward the car with* BOBBY *a few steps behind, knife at the ready.*]

BOBBY'S FATHER   She'd take your breath away, your mother. Most beautiful woman I ever saw. Snatch it out of your lungs.

Scene 13

The DOCTOR *and the* PATIENT.

PATIENT   Let's say we'd let Hal live.

DOCTOR   Okay.

PATIENT   He gives me the house and half the money, but he takes my child. That was his plan.

DOCTOR   He would have been a better father than—

PATIENT   I know that, I know that. But what about me? And even removing me as a mother from the equation, okay, then what? Hal takes the baby, I get the house. Then what? It's just the two of us, me and Will. And our love. Our love. Which doesn't seem so hot after a while if there's not a living, breathing representative of it to remind us. It's just love. Two people who fuck on Saturday night if they're not too tired from deciding where to eat the other six nights. But a child walks into the room like a candlewick? And sometimes, if you're lucky, just by looking at him you remember you were young once. You lived.

DOCTOR   We're not special.

PATIENT   I know. I know.

DOCTOR   None of us.

PATIENT   I do. I know that now.

DOCTOR   Do you?

PATIENT   Hey, I'm still getting my head around it, but . . .

[*Beat.*]

How long since your wife left you?

DOCTOR   I never said my wife left me.

PATIENT   How long?

DOCTOR   She kicked me out six months ago. She . . . met someone.

PATIENT   You let me believe I knew where you lived.

DOCTOR   Well, I do. She doesn't.

PATIENT   So she's not the perfect wife?

DOCTOR   She was never even a very good wife. But I was never even a very good husband. I love her, though.

PATIENT   Go back to her.

DOCTOR   We don't work. I mean, I mean, there's what you want and what you can do. And in between? The world fucking waits to take its bites.

PATIENT   Didn't you know that going in?

DOCTOR   Who knows that, going in? I knew the odds were a bit against us. I knew we didn't really . . . align. But what do you do with the love? Put it on a shelf?

PATIENT   Apparently, you do.

DOCTOR   Yes. Apparently.

PATIENT   Why'd you sleep with me?

DOCTOR   Because I was an asshole.

[*Chuckles. Shrugs.*]

Because pain does that.

PATIENT   It does, huh?

DOCTOR   I'm sorry. Broke-down, lost-heart sorry.

[*Beat. She smiles. She takes his face in her hands.*]

PATIENT   I want to give you something.

DOCTOR   No. No. This ends.

PATIENT   It's not that. It's not that. Trust me. Can you trust me?

DOCTOR   Not really.

PATIENT   Just this once. Pretty please?

DOCTOR   Okay, but—

PATIENT   Shush. Close your eyes.

[*He does. Long beat. She kisses each eyelid once. She steps back. His eyes remain closed for a beat. He opens them. He stares at her and she at him.*]

DOCTOR   Thank you.

PATIENT   Thank you. You probably can't be a husband, but be a father. Okay?

[*She takes several steps backward.*]

DOCTOR   What about you?

PATIENT   Oh, yeah. That.

[*She smiles and give him a bow. She waves and exits.*]

Scene 14

Lights gradually up on BOBBY'S FATHER, *his head barely above the grave now.* BOBBY *perches above the hole.*

BOBBY'S FATHER   I can't fucking . . .

BOBBY   Keep digging.

BOBBY'S FATHER   Give me a break.

BOBBY   Hard, huh?

BOBBY'S FATHER   Look, she's down here. Isn't that enough?

I admitted it. You asked, I answered. What's the point?

BOBBY   Keep digging.

BOBBY'S FATHER   But what's the fucking point?

BOBBY   Put your back into it. Use a little elbow grease. Dig, bitch. Dig.

[*BOBBY'S FATHER goes back to digging as GWEN enters. She sits behind Bobby, wraps her arms around him.*]

GWEN   Know what would be cool? If—if, if, if, if—all goes wrong? I put it in me.

BOBBY   Don't even talk ab—

GWEN   Just saying. If I swallowed it or inserted it or . . . what else?

BOBBY   You give it to him. You don't get clever. 'Member?

GWEN   The first time I saw you? Here? I swear I thought I'd lose my fucking mind if I couldn't do this . . .

[*GWEN tongues his neck.*]

Where's your father now?

BOBBY   Far away.

GWEN   Where's your life now?

BOBBY   Far away.

GWEN   Good. Gotta pee.

BOBBY   Don't go.

GWEN   Just going to the grass.

BOBBY   Don't.

[GWEN *leaves him, exits.* BOBBY'S FATHER *hits something with the shovel. Looks up.*]

BOBBY [*cont'd*]   Throw the shovel back up.

[BOBBY'S FATHER *tosses the shovel out of the grave.*]

BOBBY'S FATHER   You know, your mother and I used to come here and get ourselves some—

BOBBY   Time to whip Mom out, is it?

BOBBY'S FATHER   Get ourselves some cotton candy and ride the teacups and—

BOBBY   What was her name again?

BOBBY'S FATHER   —just feel the night. You know? You know how that feels so good, the night on you? Like to make you crazy that soft, soft touch.

[BOBBY *peers into the grave.*]

BOBBY   What'd you do with her clothes?

[BOBBY'S FATHER *looks down into the grave.*]

BOBBY'S FATHER   Burned 'em.

BOBBY   I mean, why'd you take 'em off in the first place?

[BOBBY'S FATHER *shrugs.*]

BOBBY [*cont'd*] Look at her.

BOBBY'S FATHER   I'm looking.

BOBBY   No. Look real close.

BOBBY'S FATHER   I see the bones.

BOBBY   Look closer. Where her stomach used to be. That general area.

[*BOBBY'S FATHER looks.*]

BOBBY'S FATHER   Well, I'll be damned.

[*BOBBY hits his father in the head with the shovel.*]

BOBBY'S FATHER [*cont'd*]   Now hold on—

[*BOBBY hits him again. And again. And one more time.*]

Scene 15

WILL and GINA in the parking lot.

WILL   It's a pretty color.

GINA   Are you flirting with me?

WILL   No, I just like the color. I like the blouse. I like . . .

GINA   What?

WILL   Huh? Nothing. I just . . .

GINA   Hey, you ever?

WILL   What?

GINA   Not want to get in your car?

WILL   Yeah.

GINA   When?

WILL   Now. I don't want to move.

GINA   I know.

WILL   I love that color.

GINA   Thank you.

WILL   It, um, suits you.

GINA   What suits you, Will?

WILL   You.

[*WILL touches her chin with his fingers. GINA backs away.*]

GINA   I'm married.

[*WILL shrugs.*]

WILL   You. You do, Gina.

GINA   Oh God.

WILL   Oh Something.

Scene 16

BOBBY *finishes filling in the grave. He stands in pale, weak moonlight and removes his baseball cap to wipe his brow.*

BOBBY   I wish . . . I wish . . . I wish I'd taken a picture of you. Just one. Just once.

[GWEN *enters from the darkness.*]

GWEN   You don't need a picture.

BOBBY   Yes. Yes, I do.

GWEN   No, baby, you don't. You're good.

BOBBY   Enough?

GWEN   Enough. Yeah. You're good enough.

BOBBY   I'm not. I'm not.

[GWEN *approaches until she's an inch from him and* BOBBY *recoils from the pain. Her lips pass a hairsbreadth from his ear.*]

GWEN   You are. You are.

[GWEN *fades into the dark.* BOBBY *covers his face with his baseball cap. Long beat.* BOBBY *removes the cap from his face and places it on his head. He tosses the shovel into the darkness. He takes several breaths. He notices a bench and goes to it. He sits. He pulls his cap tighter down his forehead. Music slowly filters into the scene as the light around him grows enough to reveal—*

He sits in a bar booth. A waitress emerges from the darkness. It is not the WAITRESS *we've seen before. It's* GINA/PATIENT *and she looks weary from a long night.*]

GINA   Solo?

BOBBY   Huh?

GINA   Just you tonight, sweetie?

BOBBY   Just me.

GINA   What can I get you?

BOBBY   Take a Bud and a shot of Beam.

GINA   Right back.

[BOBBY *splays his hands out in front of him and studies them. He removes his cap and runs a hand through his hair.* GINA *emerges from the dark as he rubs his face and leans back against the booth.* GINA *cocks her head, recognizing something in his movements, the jut of his jaw, his eyes. She looks at the tray in her hand. She looks at him.* BOBBY *turns his head and notices her. He smiles. She approaches.*]

BOBBY   New?

GINA   New?

BOBBY   Here. You're new here.

GINA   Um, yeah. Yeah. Yes, I am.

[*She places his drinks on the table.*]

BOBBY   What happened to V?

GINA   V?

BOBBY   Videlia. She was the waitress here for, like, centuries.

GINA   Oh, she met a man. You know. True love. Moved all the way to Coronado, way I hear it. He's a musician.

BOBBY   Big music town, Coronado? I hadn't heard.

GINA   You know how it is. It's all big music if you think you can play.

[BOBBY *throws back his shot.*]

BOBBY   And if you can't?

GINA   You find out, don't you? One way or the other.

[BOBBY *nods. He smiles at her. She smiles back. A curious, comfortably awkward beat.*]

GINA [*cont'd*] Well, I should . . .

BOBBY   Sure. You go ahead, um . . .

GINA   Gina.

BOBBY [*Offers his hand.*] Bobby.

GINA [*Shakes his hand.*] Nice to meet you, Bobby.

BOBBY   The same, Gina.

[GINA *has a little trouble letting go of his hand, but eventually she does.*]

BOBBY [*cont'd*] And, hey, Gina?

GINA   Yeah?

BOBBY   I'm thirsty as all hell tonight. Fact, I'm fixing to howl
        at the moon. So keep 'em coming, yeah?

[*GINA smiles a broken smile.*]

GINA   You bet, sweetie. But you promise me something?

BOBBY   Sure.

GINA   You let ol' Gina tell you when you've had enough.
        Okay? It's been raining nickels out there the last half
        hour. You hear it?

BOBBY   I hear it.

GINA   And the weatherman says it's going to rain all night. The
        roads get slick. Real slick. And I want you getting home.

BOBBY   Okay.

[*She nods and he nods back and she walks off into the darkness.
BOBBY spins his empty shot glass as the rain clatters on the roof.*

*A song comes on the jukebox and BOBBY watches a YOUNG
WOMAN appear and start to sway to the beat. A MAN comes up behind her, and she leans back into him. For a few moments, it's purely
sexual, and then she turns in his arms and looks straight in his eyes
and mouths the song's refrain to him, and he looks back at her, help-
less and emboldened and in love.*

Lights fade on the rest of the bar.

*BOBBY watches them with a mixture of enjoyment and envy and
heartbreak. When it gets to be too much, he turns away. He spins his*

empty shot glass again. He looks back at them and gives it all a small, sad smile. He turns back to the table, spins the shot glass.

Lights down on BOBBY.

Only the MAN *and* YOUNG WOMAN *are lit as they dance. They can't take their eyes off each other.*

Lights down on the MAN *and* YOUNG WOMAN.

The song ends abruptly.

The rain takes over, clattering . . .

. . . and faintly, the sound of BOBBY *spinning that shot glass.*

Lights out.]